The Wrench Theory

Wrench

Book 1

By Lucas Brady

Paperback: 979-8-9867076-9-3

First paperback edition October 2023

Written by Lucas Brady
Edited by Lucas Brady
Story Idea by Lukas Thompson

Printed by KDP Print in the USA

Kindle Direct Publishing
410 Terry Ave N
Seattle, WA 98109

Other books by Lucas Brady:

-Magona's Rise-

Roan
Loca
Brain

-Wrench-

The Wrench Theory

~All available on Amazon.com or most book retailers~

This book is dedicated to Lukas Thompson, who wanted to create a doppelganger story.

Table Of Contents

1

The Interview

Static appears on a television screen, glitching and sending out an ear-wrenching sound.

Through the gray lines and splotches, an almost monochrome video of two men opposite each other begins to tune in. The date March 22nd, 1989 flashes on screen in typewriter-esc font.

The man on the left, Ted Krinks, is an upright, British man with a freshly trimmed sand bowl cut atop his taller-than-wide face. He folds both of his bony hands over his square patterned orange suit pants. He licks his drained red lips, his yellow eyes bleeding through the black and white.

"Tell me, what is the Wrench theory?" he asks, his voice proper and crisp. Opposite him sits a disgruntled man, clad in a less-than-spotless white trench coat, with globs of pen ink and dirt amongst the stains. He rubs his peeling fingers into his greasy black hair, which droops down past his five-o-clock shadow. He hunches over the marble table he sits beyond.

"Well," he begins. His voice is shaky and crackly. "The Wrench theory, named after Simon Wrench who crafted it, is the idea that there are possibly people around us that look exactly like us. We call them 'doppelgangers,' for their almost identical appearance to ourselves. Now, we all know Simon Wrench died years ago attempting to discover a portal to another universe, perhaps to one that brought the doppels to us."

"Can you tell us a little more about these, doppelgangers, as you call them?" Ted politely asks.

"Yes, they are creatures, perhaps even human. They look and act exactly like us, and I mean EXACTLY. Simon Wrench explains in great detail in his unfinished memoir, Simon Says: The Story of My Life, how he came across a body near his cabin in the woods. He stated it looked exactly like him. Even down to the position of teeth. And in his theory, he states that anyone could be one and not know it."

"And how could we discover who is and isn't a doppelganger?" Ted asks, moving around some papers across the table. He picks up a white mug that reads '#1 TED' and takes a sip. He scrunches his nose. "Is there some sort of identifying trait?"

"Well," the scientist explains. "My team and the CDD are creating a device in order to scan the DNA of a person to see if that could reveal the doppels."

The television shuts off with a violent BLEEP as a man cast in shadow drops the remote on a dirty brown carpet. He mumbles under his breath as he walks past the television, the black screen reflecting a yellow plaid couch.

The sunlight from outside shines through an open window to the right of the TV, and the man walks out of the room as he slams a door behind him.

—

"Simon, you have about twenty feet before you're at the threshold."

Simon Wrench dons heavy protective gear, almost like an astronaut suit. It's heavy and white, with a glass dome for sight. He awkwardly waddles along the dry fall dirt, with leaves slowly wafting to the ground. Inside his helmet, a few screens display different aspects of both inside and outside the suit.

"Control, I can feel a change in the atmosphere," Simon says. He can see his reflection in the dome as it fogs from his breath. A fluffy black puff of hair sits on top of his head, and his thick black framed glasses enlarge his thin brown eyes.

"Just keep calm and continue," the voice from the other side responds. A streak of blue shoots right past Simon.

"Are you seeing that?" he asks.

"Yep," control adds. A few more flashes streak by Simon, who looks through the wall of trees to see some sort of pulsing orb.

"Are you picking up any new signals? I'm seeing some sort of blue light up ahead," Simon whispers. He walks into the cracking trees, where he approaches the blue orb. It's about the same size as his six-foot-eight height. He slowly raises one of his glove-covered fingers toward the orb.

"This is the energy signal, guys."

"Something's wrong with the camera," control says. "Pull back, don't eng-"

"No, let him continue," a second voice says from control. Simon recognizes it as Martin Geno's, Simon's partner at the CDD. As his finger phases through the orb, it begins to fizzle away and the voice of control glitches in and out.

"Can—you—hello?" is all Simon can hear.

"Control?" Simon calls out. He looks around as the blue streaks reverse into the dispapering orb. His body pulses as he can feel his body and soul splitting. Simon lets out a scream as the suit around him burns away, and he's disconnected from control.

2

Nine Years Later

- September 26th, 1998 -

*M*arcus Cole walks down a sidewalk with white wired headphones leading into his jean's back pocket. The sun rises in the North behind him, and the clouds above him shine orange and gray. He nods his head as he walks, sometimes half-tripping over a crack in the pavement. He holds his hands in the middle pocket of his Seventh Hunter hoodie, based on a shitty movie he enjoys to watch on the weekends.

Marcus is a roughly twenty-seven-year-old who enjoys walking in the wilderness, collecting bugs, and going on general adventures. He's a bigger guy, with a flat puff of brown hair on top of his chubby face. His smile rounds his cheeks, and pushes his sharp chin out. He's about six feet tall, and he was once recruited to be on his school's basketball team.

Since he has his eyes closed when listening to his jams, he doesn't notice Janus Peterson standing next to him. He has been for a while. Janus is twenty-eight years olds, and has known Marcus for years. He's a shorter, and skinnier, white guy with a cloud of blonde hair that circles the back of his head. He pushes up large-framed glasses, and adjusts his Dollar Double band t-shirt. Janus tries to talk to Marcus, but his music blocks him out. Janus shakes his head and taps Marcus' shoulder, which barely spooks him. He removes his headphones, and places them in his pockets as he opens his eyes.

"What did you say?" Marcus asks, his voice deep and loud. Janus shakes his head once more.

"Nothing, man, I was just asking what's up?" Janus says, his voice high and dry.

"Nothing much, y'know, I'm just walking to where we said to meet up."

"Well, you passed it." Janus says. Marcus stops and looks behind him, where he sees the black gate entrance to the local graveyard. He stops dead in his tracks.

"Right…," Marcus awkwardly sighs.

"Anyway, are you ready?" Janus asks. Marcus' left eyebrow raises, and his mouth moves to the right.

"Ready for what?" he asks. Janus' eyelids droop and his mouth flattens.

"You dumbass! Did you forget already??" Janus throws his arms out in the air and his screams alert a passing roofless crimson 1991 Miata MX-5, which seats a few attractive girls who stare at Janus as they slowly pass. Janus hopes they keep driving as his arms stay in the air and his face holds an embarrassed expression. Marcus turns his head back to see the car slowly stop at a stop sign. They all wait for a moment of awkwardness as the girls stare at Janus, stopped at the red octagon. Janus' heart stops for a moment, and the staring stops as the car continues. Marcus turns back to Janus.

"Could you remind me again?"

"We're going to find doppelgangers!" Janus yells out, throwing his arms back up. Luckily, no cars pass by this time, only the chirping of birds in the trees around them. "Like in the video I sent you."

"The video? You really think that was real?"

"Yeah, the one Barney Dorson posted on GeoCities," Janus responds. Marcus sighs.

"They're obviously not real. I mean, it wouldn't be that hard to fake."

"Believe whatever you want to, but they're definitely real," Janus says. "At least, I think they are."

"Yeah man, whatever," Marcus says. He pulls his headphones out and puts them back in his ears. "Let's just go to your house and play some games."

"I thought we were going to look for doppelgangers?" Janus asks as Marcus begins walking back the way he came. Janus throws his arms out to his side. "It's our only day off for like…a month."

"Like I said man," Marcus says, turning his head back. "Not real. Even if they were, finding our own doppelgangers would be impossible. Too big of a world."

"I guess you're right," Janus says. He catches up to Marcus and looks back. At the stop sign from before, someone stares at him. Janus shakes it off as someone from the senior center down the road.

—

"You motherfucker!" Janus yells out, throwing his expensive controller across the room. He sits on a blue bean bag, at the foot of his tall bed, where Marcus sits atop. The controller lands at the door of Janus' closet. Marcus hops up and places his on a bookcase that covers the right side of the room, opposite the door. He puts it right next to a few vinyl collectibles Janus owns, and his cheapass record player.

"You're jealous I beat you every round we played," Marcus laughs. He walks up to the curved television, and presses the power button on the back. Janus holds his head in his hands.

"This is boring, we should've gone out to find our doppelgangers, man," Janus says through his fingers. Marcus sits back on the bed, which squeaks from his weight. He stares at the blank TV screen.

"Maybe we should have," he says. "This game sucks anyways, we play it every week. Do you have anything else?"

"I mean, I have some single player games," Janus says, pulling his hands down. He adjusts himself in the beanbag. "I have Resident Evil. I've beaten that game more times than I can count...I think it has multiplayer now that I think about it."

"Nah, I got that game on my computer," Marcus says. "We need to do something. It's only twelve-thirty."

"I have an idea," Janus says. He sits up and looks at

Marcus. "Let's go out…into the beautiful weather…and look for our doppelgangers."

"For the last goddamn time, we are NOT doing that," Marcus states coldly. Janus turns around and flops down into his beanbag. He crosses his arms.

"I tried."

"I mean, we can go explore the woods down the street," Marcus suggests. "I need some new bugs to catch."

"Sure, I wouldn't mind," Janus responds.

—

"Janus, I forgot to ask you, why are your parents never home?" Marcus asks. The pair walk the dry fall path through the neighborhood forest. Orange and brown leaves make their way to the dirt, and Marcus jumps on every stick he can find. Janus kicks around leaves and ant hills, accidentally getting a few ants on his new black and red sneakers.

The air is crisp and cold, but the boys brought their matching Seventh Hunter II hoodies. It's all black with the red and green logo plastered across the front. They see a few deer roaming around the place, but no other humans.

"Their work is really important to them, so they tend to be out a lot," Janus responds.

"What do they do?" Marcus asks. "I never wanted to ask this in the past cause I didn't wanna seem rude."

"Nah, man, you're all good," Janus laughs. "I'm not allowed to tell anyone, though. It's really a secret."

"Run!" yells out a mysterious man, who jumps out

from behind a tree. The boys both scream out loud as they look upon the disgruntled man. He has long light-brown hair that's greasy and dirty, and his clothes are oil stained jean overalls and no shoes. He grabs onto Marcus' shoulders with boney fingers.

"Get out of here before it's too late!" the man yells out. He stares into Marcus' eyes with sunken brown pupils above an elongated mouth.

"Get off me!" Marcus yells, pushing the man back, who falls onto the ground. The man stares up at the twisting branches of the trees, blocking out the setting sun. He murmurs something under his breath as he pulls himself away. Marcus and Janus run the opposite way, back to Janus' house.

"What was his problem?" Janus asks.

"I don't fucking know, he's probably a crazy drug addict," Marcus responds with a shrug. They can see Janus' house down the street as they reach the end of the forest and the beginning of the neighborhood.

"Do you think he's protecting something?" Janus asks. They stop running and slow down once they hit the roads. They look around the empty, yet lived-in neighborhood as they walk down the peopleless sidewalks. People live in the houses, they just never come out.

"He's probably on drugs, man."

"He looked familiar," Janus thinks. "Like that kid that went missing a while ago."

"I didn't get a good look at him, he kind of shoved

15

himself in my face," Marcus complains. "And besides, that kid was found dead last week."

"Are you sure?" Janus asks. They turn a corner where down the street is Janus' baby blue victorian-era house. "I'm like ninety-four percent sure that was him. He had the hair and everything, his face was all over the milk crates my mom brought home."

"Yeah, I remember he was all over the news," Marcus adds. "But they found his body. It was by the old Simon Wrench cabin. There were no signs of foul play."

"Maybe I'm just seeing things then," Janus says. He looks behind him to the setting sun. "Time went by fast."

"Ya, it's getting pretty dark," Marcus responds. He looks down at his wrist where he checks the time on his black dollar store digital watch. The time displays 00:00. "Huh, my watch isn't working."

"Lemme check my phone," Janus says. He reaches into his pocket and pulls out his flip phone. He opens up the dark red shell to see the time display 00:00 and no date. "What the fuck?"

"My phone too," Marcus says, who has his updated smartphone out. They both look at each other as they slowly put their phones back into their pockets. "Maybe there's an update we missed?"

"Something weird is going on, man," Janus says. "We haven't seen a single person since we got back from the woods. No cars, no people, no nothing."

"I'm sure that's just how your neighborhood is usually," Marcus laughs. A strike of lightning scares the boys, and they both crouch down. "Let's get back to your house."

"I agree, I think it's about to rain," Janus responds. The clouds above them darken as they run to Janus' house. The homeless man watches them from the corner they turned, hiding behind a metal trash can as black unmarked vehicles drive by. He eyes them as Janus and Marcus run into the house. A drop of rain falls to the ground.

3

Momma

"Sir, now is your chance."

Martin Geno holds a flip phone to his ear as he watches over a circular screen. A live stream of somebody in the woods plays as some scientists run around the dark room with papers and clipboards. Geno wears his best black suit, complete with a blood-red tie and white napkin in his suit pocket. His pale skin shines with a singular white light above the screen.

"Send some men into the portal," Geno says, his voice demeaning and strong. His perfectly aligned teeth shine as his gleaming lips move about with each syllable. "We have plenty of men that can be used for whatever. They're in the Western wing, right under the State Bank."

"Yes sir," the voice on the phone responds. "One at a time or all at once?"

"If you do it all at once, you run the risk of someone coming back knowing that we're sending them in a death trap," Geno answers, rubbing his forehead. "Common knowledge."

"Yes sir. Right away sir."

The man hangs up, and Geno sighs as he closes his

phone and places it in his front left pocket. A scientist runs up to him and hands him a clipboard. Geno looks down to see a piece of paper with black lines criss-crossing around.

"What is this? A children's drawing?" Geno yells out.

"No, sir, it's energy readings from the orb," the scientist says. "The orb is coming back and we could have a Simon situation again."

Geno's skin turns red as the other scientists turn around. Some cover their ears and others hide behind clipboards. Geno's eyes are cast in heavy shadow as he moves under the only lightsource in the room. He places one finger on the scientist's chest.

"You mention that name again," Geno begins. He pushes his finger into the man's chest. He starts to groan as the finger breaks skin. "And I swear to God..."

Geno feels his finger rip through muscle and touch blood. He stares into the scientist's eyes with a stoic expression. His face is mostly cast in black. He quickly pulls his finger out, and the scientist falls to the ground, clutching his chest and gasping for air. On the tip of Geno's finger is a thin layer of the man's heart.

"I'll take the rest of it with me."

He storms out of the room, leaving the man to bleed out and struggle for air.

—

Janus and Marcus enter the house, the door squeaking as they walk into the main foyer. Before them is

19

a staircase up to the top floor, which is where Janus' room is. The arched door softly shuts behind them, and they shake off the rain. It's pouring outside now, and the wind is violently pulling the trees and trash and sending them down the streets. Marcus looks around at the white-walled rooms that lie on either side of him. They both carefully walk to the right room, where they enter the living room.

"Does something feel different to you?" Janus asks. He walks across the silver carpet and plops down onto the four-person wide purple leather couch. He sinks into one of the cushions. He feels around for the remote, where he clicks the television on.

"No, what do you mean?" Marcus asks in return, sitting next to Janus and looking up at the wall-mounted TV. It rests above a brick fireplace, with a small bundle of flames giving warmth to the room. Atop a mantle sits a few framed photos of Janus from different ages. The television switches onto a news broadcast.

"-any idea what you saw?" a brown haired woman asks. She wears a light gray trench coat, and faces away from the camera. The woman shoves a black microphone into a soaking wet man, who looks like he's about thirty-five. The man looks horrified, as his piss-yellow eyes are bloodshot and open wide. Bleeding scratches line his face, and one of his ears has a bite mark taken out.

"I don't know, something just…feels off," Janus responds.

"I-I saw something that l-looked just l-l-like me!"

20

the man yells out. The comment causes Janus and Marcus to jump up. They both look at each other as the man continues. "He ran off into the woods after he brutally attacked me."

Janus raises the remote and turns the TV off. He stares at the blank screen for a moment.

"It's too late to be thinking about this," he says. "I need something to eat…all this walking and doppelganger worry has gotten to my stomach."

"I'm hungry and tired," Marcus says. He pulls out his phone and taps on the screen, but it still doesn't turn on. He puts it back in his pocket. "Am I staying the night again?"

"You stay over a lot," Janus says. He stands up from the couch and places the remote next to a lamp on a dark wood table. He pulls down on the little bead to turn the yellow glow off, and adjusts the white woven lampshade.

"Yeah, there's a lot of stuff that's been going on at my house," Marcus responds. He pushes himself from the couch and the two walk past framed paintings and the staircase into the clean and shining linoleum kitchen. "I feel bad for my little brother Harry, he has to deal with it all."

"Do you want some burgers?" Janus asks, walking around the middle island and over to the silver seven-foot-tall fridge. He opens up the double doors and the cold shelves are completely empty. "Huh, that's odd."

"I would order something, but I'm a little low on cash," Marcus says, pulling out his wallet and only having a five dollar bill. Janus closes the fridge doors and looks at the marble countertops that line the walls. The normal appliances, such as the bronze toaster, are in their normal spots but the knife holder is empty, and no food remnants or random silverware can be seen.

"That's alright…," Janus says as he stares at the empty kitchen. "I think."

Janus looks around a little more, and he notices how the windows that used to be next to the fridge and above the vintage gray stove are gone. The area they used to be is covered by the baby blue floral pattern wallpaper that wraps around the kitchen.

"Marcus," Janus says. "The windows and door are gone."

"What?" Marcus asks. He looks up from attempting to activate his phone, to no avail. He sees the absent space, and looks back to the foyer, where he sees a shadowy figure lurking at the bottom of the staircase. The light from the living room is off, and only the dim yellow shine from the kitchen illuminates her white pupils. "Janus?"

Janus turns around and sees the figure, and jumps back when he does. The creature takes one step forward, and its foot is brought into the light. Janus looks down at it to see a cozy brown slipper. The figure lunges into the light, almost like a predator in the jungle. It stands up and almost towers over Marcus.

"Mom?" Janus asks. The creature is identified to be Janus' mother, Mary Peterson. Her bouncy ball of blonde hair that sits in a circle on top of her round, bright-green-eyed face. Her cheeks are soft red, which matches the shade of lipstick she wears. Her dark and light green striped sweater contrasts the orange dress pants that end right above her protruding ankles. To Janus, that's his mother but something seems off. Her limbs are slightly elongated compared to what he remembers.

"What are you doing here?" Janus asks. He stands behind the marble island. His mom walks up to it, and Marcus steps back. Mary places her hands on the island and leans over it.

"What do you mean? I live here," Mary exclaims. "This is MY house."

"You're barely ever here," Janus says, raising a finger up to his mother. "I NEVER see you anymore. I haven't seen your face in months."

"Well, I'm here now! Aren't you happy?"

"Janus, she's your mother," Marcus tries to cut in. Janus stares him down with dagger eyes.

"That," Janus points to Mary. "Is NOT my mother."

"What are you talking about, son?" Mary cries out. She spreads out her arms as if she's subtly asking for a hug. Her eyes water as her smile fades.

"You're always at 'the lab,'" Janus yells back. "You and my father are never here, and I'm always left to fend for myself. You have never been there for me."

"Son, are you feeling alright?" Mary asks. She slowly begins walking around the island toward Janus. "What is the lab? I don't work at one, I'm down with your grandmother at the senior center. Are you feeling ok? Come here, son."

She holds her arms out to Janus, who pushes her back. She wails as she crashes to the ground, her skull shattered against the tile floor. A splatter of blood squirts across the wall behind her. She lays in a ragdoll position as Janus backs up into the counters.

"YOU ARE NOT MY MOTHER!" Janus yells out. Marcus stands awkwardly in the corner.

"Why…," Mary asks. Her head twitches as her eyes roll to the back of her head. Her limbs contort and crack as she snaps herself into place. She rises to her feet, her bones sticking out from her skin, posing as if she was being hung from a bridge. "Would you do that?"

"What the hell are you?" Janus yells as Marcus screams from the sight. The creature's face melts to the bone, where bundles of skin and blood pour from its skeletal mouth. The bones are longer than human's, but just close enough to have an uncanny valley appearance. Its bent arms touch the ceiling, and its devilish fingers break through the roof.

"I'm your mother," the monster says in a distorted female voice that sounds almost computer generated. "What are you talking about?"

Its bent-backward legs storm across the tiles, and Janus runs over to Marcus and they both dive forward into the foyer. Janus, from the ground, grabs onto the coat stand next to the front door. As the creature pounces onto Janus, he angles the coat stand down, and it slices right through Mary's buttery, melting chest. The creature immediately slides down the stand as Janus and Marcus scuttle away.

"That is not your mom," Marcus says, catching his breath. Janus looks at him.

"You think?"

They both stand up and walk around Mary's corpse, slowly opening the door and booking it outside. The rain has passed, but the gray clouds are here to stay. The air feels cold and moving, leaves flow in the wind, and the sun remains covered. Janus puts his hood up, and Marcus ties his headphones around his left wrist. They walk down the wet sidewalk, still no cars or people moving about.

"Did you still want to look for doppelgangers?" Marcus asks. Janus shakes his head. "What should we do?"

"Call the police, maybe?" Janus suggests. "They might know what to do."

"We can't, our phones aren't working," Marcus reminds him. "Remember?"

"Right."

"Well I have no ideas, so I don't know what to do," Marcus says. They turn the corner on the street leading to the woods. The wind howls at the boys, and pushes them toward the forest.

"I think we should just walk and think of something," Janus suggests.

"I agree."

4

Crazy Man

"If that's not your mom, then what is it?" Marcus asks. Him and Janus rest against a sap-covered tree. They're at the entrance to the forest, where the leaves are greener and the trees less dense. Janus rests his head in his palms, trying to process the killing of his 'mother.'

"I don't know," Janus finally says. He picks his head up and his eyes adjust to the darkness. It's been a few hours, and they still haven't been able to see a single person. And the clouds haven't moved either. Marcus tosses a ball of wet leaves in the air and tries to catch it, but it plops against his face. "Maybe it took my mother's body or something."

"Should we go to my house?" Marcus cries out. "What if they took my parents? What is going on? Are we safe?"

Janus stands up and grabs Marcus by the shoulders, turning him to face each other. He raises one hand and brutally slaps Marcus across the face. Marcus lets out a 'OOO' and the hit leaves a bright red mark on his flappy left cheek.

"Get a hold of yourself!" Janus yells. He backhands Marcus across his right cheek. Marcus lets out another grunt. "You're supposed to be the calm one!"

"Why do I have to be the calm guy?" Marcus asks through puffed cheeks. His eyes water from the pain and his face reddens. "I should be able to freak out every once and a while."

"No, Marcus!" Janus yells. He shakes Marcus a few times by tugging on his hoodie. Janus' voice echoes through the trees and bounces off the wet leaves. "You're the guy who seems like he's always together but really doesn't! And he's just acting like he KNOWS what he's doing and is supposed to NEVER CRY!"

"What the hell are you talking about, man?" Marcus asks. He grabs onto Janus' arms and pulls them from his hoodie. Janus shoves his hands into his pockets. He lets out a quick 'sorry' as Marcus talks. "This isn't a movie or something you saw posted on GeoCities."

"Sorry, it does take a toll on how I perceive people," Janus responds.

"Can you just…," Marcus begins. He closes his eyes and rubs his forehead. "Stop talking? For just a little bit? You're making my brain hurt. We need to be thinking about what we should do. Both of our phones don't work, and who knows who we can trust. Especially since your mother tried to kill us."

"Yeah, I guess so," Janus says. They both think for a moment, putting their fingers to their chins and tapping their feet.

"Wait!" Marcus yells out, pointing a finger into the air.

"What? What?" Janus yells out. Marcus runs forward into the trees, looking around behind the bark and picking up every stick he can find. He crawls down onto the muddy dirt, smearing it across his freshly cleaned clothes. He puts his ear to the ground, and tries to hear something. "Did you think of something?"

"You remember that crazy man from earlier?" Marcus asks. He picks himself up and runs a few more feet into the treeline. As they get deeper into the forest, a blue tint lights the distance. Janus reluctantly follows behind.

"Uh, yeah, how could I forget him," Janus asks as he leisurely walks behind Marcus, who looks as though he is practicing ninja skills. He keeps jumping up and hiding behind trees, looking out for something.

"Maybe he knows what's going on," Marcus suggests. Janus shrugs.

"Maybe. But how are we going to find him? We just happened to stumble across the guy. It's not like he's gonna pop out of nowhere."

Janus stops and looks around with wide eyes as if the crazy man was going to jump out at that moment. He watches as a few leaves fly around and the wind groans at him. He shakes it off and continues to follow Marcus. They head pretty deep into the forest, where the trees grow thicker and taller. Leaves are completely withered away, and the dirt is uneven and dry.

"Crazy man!" Marcus yells out, cupping his hands around his mouth to further the reach of his voice. "Where are you at! We need to talk to you!"

Janus shakes his head as he leans against a tree. Marcus crouches in the middle of a tree circle, and calls out in every direction. The trees around him contort and bend into the middle, where they rise up like a triangle. Marcus rolls around in the dirt, his hoodie picking up leaves and dead bugs.

"Crazy man! Oh, crazy man!"

Janus holds his head with two fingers and goans.

"I don't…think he's going to answer to 'Crazy Man,'" Janus complains. He throws out his hands and his eyebrows bow to the middle of his face. Spit flies from his mouth as he yells. "Can't we just…go back? Go to your house?"

Marcus stops calling and his face grows disappointed. He stands up and wipes some crap from his clothes. A little orange and brown centipede crawls into his hoodie from the collar. He stares at Janus with one eyebrow raised and puts his hands on his hips.

"Well, I really need to talk to the crazy man-"

"HELLO, BOYS!" the crazy man yells out. He jumps down from the twisted vines above the boys and lands in front of Marcus. He lands on his feet and slips backward, crashing to the ground with a yell. Marcus screams and jumps, and Janus is visibly scared. The greasy-haired crazy man holds his back as he groans from the pain. "Ah, fuck! I'm getting too old for this shit!"

Marcus runs forward and helps the man to his feet. He pats Marcus' shoulder and pulls the hair from his face. A gross, yellow smile cracks across his dingy face.

"Were you calling me?" he asks in a croaky voice. He lets out a little chuckle that vibrates one of his front teeth, which is extremely loose. Marcus looks into the man's brown mouth, where a few teeth have been chipped away and little brown hairs stick out from his tongue. Even his tongue has dandruff.

"Yeah," Marcus says, swatting the air as he tries to waft the man's warm, toxic breath away. "We need to ask you a few questions."

"Well, just follow me, and we can discuss this over some nice porridge," the man exclaims. He stumbles past Marcus, hunched over and holding his back as Marcus and Janus exchange glances.

"Should we really be following this man?" Janus asks as he walks toward Marcus. Marcus shrugs. They both look back to the crazy man who grunts with every step.

"I mean, what's the worst that can happen?" Marcus asks. Janus stares at Marcus with a dumbfounded expression. Janus points to his head and pokes himself a few times.

"Dude!" Janus yells out as he pokes his head. "He could totally just kidnap and kill us, man!"

"Man," Marcus groans. "You gotta stop worrying so much."

Janus looks past Marcus to the crazy man, who sticks his hand deep into his oil-stained jeans. He rubs his hand a bit and then takes it out and smells the tips of his fingers. His body shivers as he does. Janus and Marcus can hear him moan from yards away. Marcus looks back at Janus.

"Ok, we can go, but if anything suspicious happens, it's on you," Janus commands. He sticks a finger in Marcus' face. "You hear me?"

"Yeah, yeah, yeah," Marcus whispers. "Listen, your mother just turned into some H.R. Giger bullshit, and your doppelganger theory is turning out to be a little close to reality. You may be able to find your doppelgangers afterall."

"Fine," Janus reluctantly says after a moment of thinking. "But if we die, I will kill you in hell."

"Like you could beat me up," Marcus says, towering over Janus' tinier build. Janus shakes his head and walks past Marcus. "You can believe whatever you want, but if anything happens, I can get out of any situation."

"Whatever, dude," Janus says as he catches up to the crazy man, but also keeps his distance. He can smell the must and grime from the stranger. "Just keep up."

5

Simon

Black trees wrap around each other, and the dry atmosphere instantly grabs any sign of water and bleeds it dry. Wind whispers in people's ears, and the clouds hang over the hill that holds up a wood cabin.

Janus, Marcus, and the stranger approach the steep hill, where the trees split and circle the mound. A soft yellow light emitting from a candle in one of the windows glows and flickers as the wind caresses the flame. A chimney atop the flat roof puffs out dark smoke, which blends into the low clouds.

"Hey, crazy man," Marcus asks. "What is this place?"

"Oh please," the man responds. He shakes his head and stands in front of the two boys. "You can call me Barney. It'll help. This is my house, at least, the house I stayed in after I found myself here."

Barney turns and begins to climb up the hill toward the cabin, and Janus leans over to Marcus' ear.

"I thought he was homeless," he whispers.

"So did I," Marcus responds. "We may actually

have a legitimate lead on your whole doppelganger-finding fantasy."

"I'm just not...too sure about this," Janus says. He leans away from Marcus' ear and looks up at the comforting cabin. The air seems to glow around the hill, as opposed to the stabbing winds of the dense black surrounding forest.

"We'll be fine," Marcus says, trying to comfort Janus. "We'll just go in...see what he has to say...and then we can leave."

"Ok," Janus says. "Let's go."

The front door creaks as Janus slowly pushes it open. He peeks in through the crack to see a small area with a yellow plaid couch sitting in front of a vintage 50s television. A yellow candle atop a small circular table illuminates the room. The brown carpet is stained with coffee and curdled milk, and the smell matches the sight. Janus takes one step into the cabin, and his foot sinks into a moist red and blue tribal design carpet. It's scratched up from some sort of animal, and the marks dig deep into the wood below.

"What is this place?" Janus whispers. He looks to the left where he sees a dark room where a soft hum is being emitted from the darkness. Janus takes a few steps toward the room, and Marcus follows behind. As Janus walks, Marcus watches his back and sees a shadow appear against the wall in the right room. Janus steps out from the wood-walled corridor into the lightless room where the air turns still and Janus' breath appears in a frosty glow before his mouth.

"Uh, Janus?" Marcus asks as the shadow glides across the wall, and a wide figure squeezes through the doorway. His body blocks the candle light behind him. Janus reaches forward and feels a patch of cold skin. It feels human.

"There's someone in here," Janus says as the lights suddenly click on, and the boy's eyes take a moment to adjust and they both groan from the brightness. As Marcus blinks his eyes a few times and looks at the door, he sees Barney standing to the left side with his hand below a lightswitch. As Janus wipes his eyes and opens them, he sees a mangled body tied up to a metal chair with torn rope. Janus lets out a scream that scares Marcus.

"I knew this was a trap!" Janus screams out. He backs into Marcus, who watches as a square man bends down to enter the room. Janus looks around at the garage he finds himself in, with tools and weapons hanging on the walls, silver tool benches holding saws and traps, and smears of blood across the floor.

"Who are you people?" Marcus yells out. The man steps into the light, and he is lit up from the singular bulb hanging by a wire from the ceiling. He's a brick of a man, with fluffy black hair atop his rectangular face. Black, thick framed glasses sit comfortably on his blocky nose. His cheeks are a rosy color, and they squish his blue lips together. He dons a black suit, which has been covered and ruined by stains and dirt.

"Hello," the man says in a brooding and demanding voice. "Seems like Barney brought new friends with him."

"I think I hear my mother calling me," Marcus says, pulling out his broken phone and pointing to its black screen. "I better get going...she may kill me if I'm late to supper!"

"Oh, you're not going anywhere," the man demands. He blocks the door with his extreme build. Janus cries out as he falls to his knees in front of the body.

"Oh God!" he yells out. "I knew we were going to be killed! I just knew it!"

"What do you mean we aren't going anywhere?" Marcus asks, trying to puff out his flabby chest to seem imposing. The man grabs onto Marcus' head and his hand is the same size as Marcus' face. The man pulls him up and stares into Marcus' eyes.

"I mean that you aren't going anywhere," he states. Marcus scrunches up into himself and squints his eyes as he turns his head away.

"Are you going to kill us?" he asks in a horrified and squeaky tone. The man squints his eyes and pulls Marcus close to his face. Marcus gets a good look at the man's sunken brown eyes.

"Kill you?" he coldly whispers. He lets go of Marcus, who falls to the floor and bangs his head against Janus' foot. "No. You aren't going anywhere because...I haven't finished dinner yet!"

"What?" Janus and Marcus both ask, looking at each other. The man's blocky and towering demeanor fade as he lets his stomach hang out and unstraightens his back. Him and Barney both exchange a high-five.

"You both must be starving from the walk here," Barney laughs. "I know I am."

He makes a circular motion with his hand over his stomach. Marcus does the same as he imagines some good food.

"Well, I'll be done in a bit, so make yourselves at home," the man says. He leans backward as he steps out the room. Barney walks over to the boys and helps them to their feet. He helps them past the living room and into a dining room, where a dusty table holds five chairs around its angled shape. One of the chairs is missing a leg, and is being held up by a few leather-bound books. On the walls, paintings of red and black figures hang between empty wine racks. The colors of the room are mostly corduroy brown, metal gray, and the candles shine a bright yellow.

The smells of the room are more decent than the living room, with the scent of spoiled milk nonexistent. Behind the table a large window lines the wall and the view is of the top of the forest. Some trees reach up higher, but most are pretty low. The clouds make the dense forest pretty murky looking. Janus takes a seat on one of the chairs, and Marcus sits opposite him. Barney sits between the two. He places four mugs on the table, and they wipe away the dust. Janus picks one up and looks in, but it's empty.

"So, you guys need something?" Barney asks. He takes a sip from his empty mug.

"Oh yeah," Marcus pipes up. "So, things have been feeling really off recently."

"Off, ok," Barney repeats. He crosses his legs and rests his chin on his fist.

"We were wondering if you knew anything about this," Marcus says as he pulls out his phone and slides it to Barney. "They won't turn on."

"Did you charge it?" Barney asks as he picks up the phone and examines it. "It looks dead."

"That's the thing, it's not just my phone," Marcus says. He points to Janus. "It's his phone too. And we haven't seen any signs of life for the past day. And his mother tried to kill us after turning into some monster."

"Some monster, you say?" Barney asks. He places the phone down and slides it across the dusty table. He leans over to get closer to Marcus. "What did it look like?"

"It looked like my mother, and acted like her too until I accidentally killed her," Janus explains. "And then she contorted and turned into some...creature."

"So, you haven't found out yet?" Barney asks. He leans backward into his chair.

"Found out what?" Janus asks. The wind outside bangs on the window, which frightens the two boys. Barney remains unmoved.

"This isn't your home," Barney says.

"Well, duh, this is yours," Marcus responds. Barney shakes his head and crosses his arms.

"No, I mean home as a general place, not a house," he explains further. "Do you know anything about the multiverse? Or cross-dimensional travel?"

"Yeah, I think I saw it in a movie one time," Janus says.

"Multiverse? What does this have to do with anything?" Marcus asks. His face is perplexed, and his tone of voice matches. Barney chuckles.

"The multiverse is a theory in which there are infinite other universes that all stem from one center point in time in the middle of all universes," Barney explains. "And the cross-dimensional theory is a topic about how to breach time and be able to enter one of these other universes."

"Please, that's all just a bunch of nonsense," Marcus cuts in. "There's no such thing as a multiverse. It's just some shit you see in superhero movies."

"Then how do you explain where you are?" Barney asks.

"What?" Marcus asks. "What the fuck are you talking about?"

"Dude," Janus says, his face frozen in shock as he realizes what Barney means. Marcus looks over to him. "It makes sense. Think about it, man. We're in another universe, that's why our phones don't work and why my mother was some creature."

"Seems like you're the smart one," Barney says to Janus. Janus lets out a hearty laugh.

"Not at all," Janus and Marcus both say, Janus laughing and Marcus serious.

"It's not possible," Marcus continues. He rubs his fingers through his brown hair. "It can't be, it's all just fiction."

"It's real whether you like it or not," Barney adds. He takes another sip from his empty mug. Janus looks back into his and still sees nothing.

"Is there a way to get back into our universe?" Marcus asks. "We could just walk out the way we came."

"It's complicated," Barney says. He draws something in the dust with his finger. He doodles two stick figures, one skinny and one large. "Both the big guy and I are both from the same dimension. Your dimension."

He draws a circle surrounded by stick trees.

"Sometimes, I can exit but I can only walk so far until I'm pulled back in. I tried to stop you, but you both ventured too far."

"And what about the guy you tied up?" Janus asks. Barney looks up as he sketches a large globe that looks like Earth. Barney licks his dry lips, picking up a few skin flakes.

"He's one of 'them,'" he says. Marcus leans onto the table and rests his head on his arm.

"One of 'them?'" Marcus asks. Barney nods his head. He leans back and picks up a candle from a counter behind him. He holds onto the melting wax with his bare fingers. His dirty long nails dig into the candle as he places it on the dusty table.

"They're zombie-like creatures," he begins. "They come from this world, but I'm not sure how. There's tons of them, especially in the surrounding forest. They come out when the candle melts all the way down."

Janus stares at the candle which is about halfway melted. He gulps as the flame dances around.

"And you have one in your garage?" Marcus asks. "What if he comes alive and kills us?"

"Don't worry," Barney laughs. "He's definitely dead. They are not hard to kill, you just have to know they'll come back once."

"Why don't you throw him out?" Janus asks.

"We keep him for research to know what these…things…are," Barney explains.

"Dinners ready!" the brick man says as he enters the room with four plates. He holds two in his hands and has two on his shoulders. He sets the two in his hands down onto the table, and lets the other two slide down. Barney adjusts his plate so that the main meal is closest to him.

"Anyway, that's enough talking," Barney says as the man crashes onto the broken chair. "Let's get to eating."

Janus looks down at his plate, where a large slab of tenderized and seasoned meat glistens next to a bowl of boiled porridge mixed with zucchini bites. He picks up a bent fork from his plate and stabs it into the meat.

—

- 11 Years Ago -

Simon Wrench crashes through a wooden door. He falls to the ground, onto a red and blue tribal patterned carpet. He gasps for air as his oxygen tank depletes, and he tries to remove his suit. He twists and turns the helmet, but one of the pegs is stuck in the exit button. His skin turns purple as his vision begins to go. He pulls himself forward by grabbing the wooden planks.

He smashes his head against the ground, and a crack forms in the glass. It does it a few times more, which shakes his brain around and gives him a headache. His fluffy black hair droops down onto his face, blocking his eyes. His screams are muffled by the glass, which finally shatters as he crashes his face into a plank. Glass shards fly into his face, and the blood drips onto the wood. He finally gets the air he needs, and his bloodshot eyes return to normal.

As he stumbles across the house and takes a seat at a perfectly set table with five newly crafted chairs, he opens one of the many pockets along his suit and pulls out a pen and a few pads of paper.

"It was a mistake opening that portal," he groans to himself. "I knew it was…and Geno did too. That bastard!"

He slams the paper onto the table and begins to

write violently. He speaks aloud as he does.

"I need to find a way out of this place. I can't be here, I need to get back home. I need to get back to my family. Oh, Jesus…what is my boy going to do? My sweet boy Janus…what is he going to do without his father? His mother can't take care of him alone…he's a little boy. I need to get back…but how?"

He thinks for a minute about his research and experience with the portal. He puts the pen back on the paper.

"If anyone reads this, the portal is like a one-way mirror. You can see it from any natural world, but it's invisible here. It moves around and appears and disappears whenever it wants, it has a mind of its own. If this portal continues to build and rage on, it can tear more entrances to this world. I need to close the portal, even if it means I'm stuck here. I can't risk anyone else going through and being trapped like me. I've only been here for what's felt like a few days, and my psyche is going crazy. I'm being corrupted, I can see it in my veins. My blood is turning purple, and my mind is going blank. If I can't close this portal, my entire world is going to be killed."

—

"Before I forget," the man at the table says through chewing his steak. He pulls out a vile from his suit pocket. "Take this."

"What's this?" Janus asks as the man hands him the vile. He opens it up and inside is a bubbly purple liquid. It pops and crackles as Janus stares his eyes down it. The man wipes his mouth with a white handkerchief from his pants pocket.

"This world is corrupted," the man explains. He pulls up his left sleeve to reveal pink scars and chunks of skin removed from his arm. Lavender veins pulse around the torn muscle. "If you stay in it long enough, parasites in the air insert your body and fly into your bloodstream. I call them the S-12 Virus, for the amount of spectolograms they hold, which is basically venom for cells."

Janus downs half the vile, and he coughs from the bitter taste. He scrunches up his face and shakes his head. He hands it to Marcus, who has no problem drinking it in sips. To him, it tastes like medicinal grapes.

"The food was amazing," Marcus says after swallowing the last of the liquid. "Where'd you learn to cook?"

"Well, when you're stuck here for twenty plus years, you gotta learn how to adapt," the man responds with a hearty laugh. He holds his stomach as it shakes from laughter.

"So, what is this place?" Janus asks.

"Well," the man begins as he takes a sip from his full mug. Janus notices his has some steaming tea in it now. "I call it the Doppel Earth, since it's an almost-perfect copy of our own. It's the only alternative universe that I've been able to study. So far, us four are the only normal humans here. Everyone else is some sort of zombie-creature-thing. I used the blood from some of the doppelgangers I've found and made that antidote to the corruption. Well, it doesn't stop the virus, it just slows it down to a snail's pace."

Janus pulls up his hoodie sleeves and sees a soft purple hue under his skin. He gulps and looks back up.

"Now, listen. There's a few places here that are woven in with our Earth," the man explains. "One of them is the forest you both entered. When you ventured deep enough, you were in the same location split across two dimensions. You walked past the barrier, which caused you to travel to this world."

"Are there any other places that are like that?" Janus asks. "Could they be the way to get back to our world? If we break the barrier into OUR world, we could escape here, right?"

"There's only one other place that I know has a barrier like that," the man sighs. "And it's heavily guarded."

6

Janus

"This is the place," the man says. On the far edge of the forest, on the complete other side of where Janus and Marcus entered, a military-esque building sits still amongst the howling wind. Its dark gray exterior drips with water, and the lack of windows gives it the appearance of a prison. A black, gothic fence weaves in and out of the curving trees, and a mud path leads up to the building's black-frosted glass doors. Two masked guards in all black man the front doors, holding customized assault rifles with crimson bowie knives attached to their hips.

"What is this?" Janus asks. The four boys hide behind a fallen log on the side of the road. They're only a few yards away from the gate. The man holds up a pair of binoculars up to his face as he scans the building.

"This is the CDD headquarters," the man explains.

"What's that?" Marcus asks. The man slowly lowers the binoculars and looks to Marcus.

"You don't know what the CDD is?" he asks. Marcus shakes his head. "It's a scientific research center, and I used to work there. I was the lead investigator for doppelganger activities. My research led me to discover so much…and it was all thrown away when I ended up here."

"Wait a minute," Janus says. The man turns his head toward Janus, handing Marcus the binoculars. "Are you Simon Wrench? The famous scientist who came up with the Wrench Theory?"

"Yes, I am," he responds. "I guess I never introduced myself properly."

Marcus watches as the guards swap out for another two. They enter through a door on the right-most section of the building. He notices a vent entrance hidden behind some decorative foliage. He whispers to Barney and points to the vent. Barney gives a nod of confirmation.

"So the CDD is real?" Janus asks. "I thought it was just stuff of legend. It's always mentioned but you can't Google the location or who runs it."

"That's cause the man who runs it is a bastard," Simon says through clenched teeth. On top of the building, a third worker appears with a flashlight. He shines around the forest, and the four boys duck behind the log if he points it their way. The binoculars are passed back to Simon. "He sent me to this world knowing I wouldn't come back. I spent so long trying to plan revenge on him, but I found it wasn't worth it. I decided there's no point in revenge if I can't escape this place."

The man atop the roof turns around, and Simon points forward with two fingers. The group hops over the log and crawls through the grass and vines. They approach the gate as someone watches them from afar. A man sits motionless, hidden behind a cracked black tree. He waits and watches them weave through the bent fences. He's been watching them ever since he followed Janus and Marcus into the forest.

———

- EARLIER -

Janus Wrench enters his house. The door creaks on his way in. The candles have been blown out by a violent gust of wind that follows behind him. He adjusts his baggy jean overalls as he runs his thin fingers through his bouncy brown hair. He looks down at the bloody corpse on the ground, recognizing it as his own mother.

He drops to the ground, holding onto his mother's pale arm. He feels the coldness of her skin, and looks into her unmoving eyes. The crimson blood around her has already dried, and Janus peels some off. Her fingernails have bent into the skin underneath, and bones stick out from her elbows.

"Mother?" Janus asks. The woman speaks nothing. He doesn't cry at all, and his voice is calm and steady. "Mother, who did this to you?"

A crash of thunder erupts through the house, and Janus jumps up. The front door hangs wide open, and Janus leaps over the split coat hanger. He dives out into the foggy street, where he sees two figures walking away in the distance. Their black silhouettes are illuminated every time a strike of lighting crashes in the distance. The odd thing, however, is that Janus feels as though only he can feel the storm. None of the trees or fallen leaves react to the sudden bursts of air and roars of thunder. Only Janus can sense it.

Janus watches the duo from afar, quietly avoiding crunchy leaves, as he sneaks up to them. He climbs into the trees, tip-toeing along the vines and branches as he stalks Janus Peterson and Marcus Cole, who are still unknown to him. He watches as the two boys pass between a dense line of trees, where blue streaks whisk through the bark. One slithers up Janus Wrench's leg, and he tries to swat it away as it cuts his leg open and slides inside. He covers his mouth to not scream as the light climbs under his skin. He feels it enter into his brain, where it overtakes his vision.

He appears in the center of the forest that he was just overlooking, with the yellow sun shining profusely down onto the lush green field. Janus Wrench looks around as he hears footsteps running toward him from a distance. He looks down a row of bright trees to see himself as a small child. Young and curious, his short brown hair whisks in the wind. His younger self wears the red and gray coat and jeans that he would constantly have on.

"Hurry, mom!" he yells out, his voice so young and high-pitched. He jumps in a pile of freshly fallen orange leaves, which all scatter around the grass. "I want to play in the woods!"

"Sorry, hon, I was trying to find my coat," a woman says as she catches up to young Janus with her arms crossed. It's his mother, Mary Wrench, who Janus just found dead moments before. "Don't you think it's a little cold here?"

She wears a fluffy brown trench coat with animal fur along the collar. The wind tosses her curly hair around, blocking her face from Janus. This is his memory of these same woods from years ago, right before his mother disappeared. Present Janus looks around as the memory continues, seeing the blue lights hide behind trees. They have a mind of their own.

"I want to play in the woods!" young Janus exclaims as he throws a few leaves in the air. Both young and present Janus turn to their mother to see she's gone. Two spots of dirt in the ground mark where she just was.

"Mom?" they both say at the same time. Present Janus feels the light grow closer to his ear as the memory fades.

"Gone."

7

The CDD

*J*anus Wrench watches closely as the four guys sneak through the front gate, narrowly avoiding the gazes of the multiple armed guards outside the building. He follows closely behind, hiding underneath rocks and tall grass to avoid anyone's gaze.

Simon and his group reach the right-most side of the building, where Janus noticed the vent earlier. Barney leans down and slides his fingers behind the grates, struggling to pull it off. He manages to bend it toward him, and he steps aside for Simon to fully tear it from the wall. The screws bounce along the pavement, and the boys look around to make sure nobody heard.

Simon enters first, and he barely fits. Janus follows behind, then Marcus, then Barney. They travel a maze of dark and dusty ventilation shafts, going in circles, dead ends, and crossing over grates. A few of them overlook dingy offices, clean testing chambers, and even an employee bathroom.

Simon leads the way until they reach a dead end, this time with a vent exit in front of them. He pushes the bottom, looking down into the room below. He sees two guards sitting on a red leather couch enjoying some coffee. They sit behind a reception desk, decorating with a typewriter, 50s computer, and a stack of sticky notes. Simon reaches both arms down and grabs onto the guard's heads, slamming them together. The guards let out a grunt as they both fall to the ground, and their mugs spill hot coffee across the black and white tile floor.

Simon crawls out of the vent, collapsing onto the couch below and causing it to split down the middle. Janus comes out next, and falls onto the left side of the couch. He bounces off and crashes onto the floor. Simon stands up and dusts off his pants, picking up Janus and dusting his shoulders. Marcus slides out with ease, carefully dropping down onto the fallen couch cushions. He joins the other three as they watch Barney exit, flipping over onto his back as he misses the couch completely.

"Are you ok?" they all ask. Barney shoots up a thumbs up as the rest of his body lays like a ragdoll. Simon turns and examines the rest of the room, recognizing it as the staircase lobby. He checks out two doors, one to his left and one directly in front of him. Two signs above both doors read 'STAIRWELL' and 'HALLWAY.'

"Just follow me guys, and we won't get lost," Simon says. He walks through the metal push door to the stairwell, which leads to a claustrophobic tunnel that angles down, seemingly forever. Before they pass through the door, they hear some chatter from behind the

'HALLWAY' door. Janus quickly hops over the counter, hiding behind it. He grabs Barney's legs and pulls him over.

"Hide!" Marcus whispers. He crawls under the couch, holding the broken frame up so that it seems fixed. Simon stays in the stairwell, holding the door closed with the handle on the other side. Marcus drags the two unconscious guards' bodies under the couch with him.

"Why do you think the boss wanted us to go down to the stairwell?" a guard asks another as they walk into the room. The four boys stay completely still and quiet, and Marcus holds his hands over the mouths of the other guards. The two that walk in wear the same outfit as the two under the couch; a blue hard hat, a clean white button down and light gray pants.

"There might be more people to recruit down there," the other guard responds. "It helps having two versions of the same building. More holding areas for those creepy doppels."

Simon hears all of this from the other side of the stairwell door.

"They're sending people through the barrier to here, and sending doppels to our world," Simon whispers to himself. The two guards walk up to the stairwell door, and Janus peeks over the counter. They begin to push the door open, and Janus' eyes widen and he takes a big gulp. The door swings open, and Simon's large figure greets the guards.

"Hey!" the first guard yells. He grabs an assault rifle from his back and points it at Simon. "What are you doing here? This is CDD property! You are trespassing on private sections which are punishable by law!"

"Well, hey," Simon says, trying to think of a good escape plan. "Are there really laws here in this doppel world? I mean, if you drag me to the barrier and send me to the normal world, thus automatically causing me to trespass, wouldn't that be on you?"

The guards both look at each other with dumbfounded expressions. Simon awkwardly smiles as he slowly shrugs his shoulders. The second guard turns his head back and takes a walkie-talkie from his belt. He puts it up to his mouth.

"Hey, I got-," he begins, but Simon quickly grabs his head and snaps it to the right. The sound of broken bones echoes through his ears. He slams the dead body into the first guard, who topples over and rolls down the stairs. Simon runs back into the room, and yells out at the others.

"We need to go!" he calls out. "NOW!"

Janus and Barney jump out from the counter and Marcus stands up with the couch still on his back. It slides off as he runs through the door with the others, jumping over the two guard's bodies and rushing down the stairwell. As they run, Barney picks up the guard's walkie-talkie.

"What's going on over there?" a voice asks from

the walkie. Barney puts it up to his mouth, a little too close.

"Oh, nothing!" he improvises. "Nothing is wrong, don't send anyone here, we have it all under control."

They run as fast and as far as they can until the stairs even out into the floor, and the cold, wet gray walls transform into fake wood and the pavement ground grows tiles. They enter down into the basement floor, where rows of halls look as though they repeat on and on, twisting and turning with no signs of direction. They make an executive decision to go the right way, where after turning a few identical brown corners, they run into a suited man. He looks away from the group, and as they get closer, Janus feels his head pulse.

"Who are you?" Marcus asks. The man doesn't respond. His fluffy brown hair flows in the wind, just like Janus'. "Do you guys know who that is?"

"I have no idea who that is," Simon responds. The man takes a step backward, toward the group. "And now he's walking backwards."

With each step, Janus' headache worsens. He groans in pain as he throws his hands up and grabs onto his pulsing hair. He shuts his eyes and hurls over.

"What's wrong?" Marcus cries out as he notices Janus.

"MY HEAD!" Janus yells. He falls to the ground, wiggling around as he holds his head. "IT HURTS!"

"We need to get him out of here!" Simon yells

back. The man takes another step backward. He quickly scoops up Janus and tosses him over his shoulder. They backtrack the way they came, but accidentally take a wrong turn and end up in some sort of endless hallway. The buzzing yellow fluorescent lights above flicker as they pass by identical metal doors, with the light at the end never seeming closer.

"Are we in some sort of loop?" Marcus yells out. "Shouldn't we try a door?"

"There might be a staircase at the end of this corridor!" Simon reassures them. His shoes clank against the tiles, and Janus lays unconscious on his shoulder. Simon squints his eyes, and a door at the end of the hall slowly comes into view. "See! It's right there!"

They all lean forward to increase their speed, and as they reach the door, it opens up on its own, and the group all trips forward and slides through into a grimy chamber. The floor is slippery and moldy, with the smell not helping. Simon pushes Janus off his shoulder and he rolls over onto his stomach. Marcus helps Barney up, and they both lift up Simon by his arms. Barney struggles to do so. On the opposite side of where they just entered lies another door, locked up with chains.

Around the walls hang torn, scarred, or shattered frames that hold portraits and paintings of Geno's family. Headshots of thin, malnourished characters that have the complexity and shaping of a skeleton wearing clothes. Smeared blood around the walls read 'DISAPPOINTING' and 'I WILL MAKE YOU PROUD.' The corners of the room contain piled-up grease and crap. Simon walks around the room, dragging his hand along the dirt-covered floral wallpaper. He looks up at the ceiling, which stretches miles up into a white light, which shines down on the four.

"What is this place?" Marcus asks, running around the empty floor. The door slowly shuts, and the room shines brighter. The paintings float down on the wall, and Simon pulls his hand away. The frames reveal little cubbies behind them, about the size of a curled-up adult. The three conscious men turn their heads around the room as the paintings come to a screeching halt, inches above the floor. Above each hole is a sign, white block letters printed on emerald street signs.

"They're all sections of the CDD," Simon says. He points to one of the signs, above a painting of Geno's Tim Burton-esque father. "That one says 'Broadcast Room.'"

"Well, we can probably use that to set a distraction for the building," Marcus suggests. "We could tap into the walkie-talkies, too."

"Yeah, we can try something," Simon responds. "Let's go."

He motions with his hands toward the hole, where they take turns climbing up. Simon carries Janus on his back as they crawl through the cobweb-covered corridor. Spiders crawl along the walls, and as the three push themselves forward with their arms, they crush roach eggs on the ground. After a few minutes of crawling, they reach a wooden trapdoor. Simon pushes it forward, and they all exit the musty path into a small room with a wall covered in screens, computers, and speakers.

8

Waking Up

"When is he going to wake up?" Marcus asks.

"When he feels like it, man," Simon responds. Marcus paces the room, worrying about Janus. "Can you calm down?"

"I can't!" Marcus yells out. "What if he doesn't wake up?"

"Just...calm down," Barney says, holding his arm out in front of Marcus. He stands leaning against the wall, next to a black file cabinet. Marcus notices one of Janus' eyes twitch, and his mouth opens. Marcus rushes over to Janus, who lies down on a metal desk.

"Janus?" Marcus asks slowly. Janus' eyes open, and he looks around. He sees the brightly lit screens, showing black and white camera views of all across the CDD. The walls are a light gray, with the single lightbulb hanging by the ceiling shattered, and its pieces along the floor. Grime hangs down from where the walls meet the ceiling, and a single wooden door across from the desk. Its golden knob reflects the screens.

"What happened...to me?" Janus asks. Barney

walks over and stands behind Marcus. "Did we get away?"

"We're deep within the CDD, Janus," Simon says. He leans against the desk, folding his arms over his chest. Janus sits up, and looks over at Marcus, who wipes sweat from his forehead.

"How long have I been out?" he asks. Marcus shrugs.

"There's no clock in here," he responds. The walkie-talkie on Barney's waist glitches on, and a voice comes through the static. Barney quickly unlatches his from his belt and puts it up to his ear.

"Have you secured the CDD yet?" says Geno, whose voice is barely recognizable. He sounds worried, yet calm and composed.

"Sir!" another voice yells through static. "The CDD—they're everywhere! Please send—to us! We need more men, we're—overrun!"

Screams come through from the walkie, and the connection fizzles out. Barney turns his eyes up to look at Simon, who shakes his head and places his head on his face.

"What's going on down there?" Geno asks. "I'm closing off the bottom floor, so save yourself."

"Are we on the bottom floor?" Marcus whispers to Simon.

"No, we're on the bottom floor but there's a basement," Simon explains. "It was meant for cryogenic freezing, and habitual simulations."

"And what was kept down there?" Marcus asks.

"Sir!" another voice says from the radio. Simon turns around and looks at the cameras, where the bottom right one displays the hallway leading into the basement stairs. Through the static and compression, two guards run through the metal staircase door, covered in blood and wailing their guns wildly. One of them holds up a radio, and his voice comes from the one Barney has. "The doppelgangers we were keeping! They—they escaped!"

"What?" Martin Geno's booming voice asks. "What did you do?"

The two guards bang on the opposite door, trying to get out of the hallway as the staircase door slowly creaks open, with a black figure crawling out. The guards turn their heads and back up against the door, as the creature rushes on all fours at them, tearing their throats out from their stomachs. The monster throws the blood and gore around the room, painting the walls as the camera feed glitches out into static.

"More men are on their way!" Geno says over the walkie. The four men stare at the camera in horror and disbelief, their eyes wide and their mouths open. Barney drops the walkie onto the ground. Simon sighs as he slams his palm on his forehead.

"Shit!" Simon cries. "We're trapped."

"Wait, why?" Janus asks, turning his head.

"Martin Geno is here," Simon responds. "We were partners here…and he betrayed me."

"Betrayed you?" Marcus asks. "You mean he killed you?"

"Well," Simon cuts in. "It's a long story."

"How come Geno isn't more in the spotlight if he took over your role?" Janus asks. Barney leans against the wall, looking slightly away. Simon sighs and pulls a rolling chair from under the desk, taking a plump seat right on it. The chair is pushed down from his weight.

"Well," he begins. "It was September twenty-fifth, nineteen-seventy-eight."

9

A Story of Friends

Geno enters the room, noticing Simon standing over his circular screen. It displays a CRT feed of a forest clearing, where some sort of organic orb pulses around. Simon is completely locked in, and doesn't even notice Geno enter. No one else is in the room since it's their lunch break. The single light above Simon illuminates only him and the screen, and Geno steps out of the shadows.

"Hello, Simon," Geno says, placing his hand on Simon's tailored black suit. Simon jumps, and turns his head back. Geno's chiseled face and pronounced cheekbones cast heavy shadow on his face, as do his overbearing eyebrows. A mole sits on the left side of his face, next to his lips. He removes his hand and slowly walks to the other side of the screen, looking down at the monochrome video.

"I've done it, Geno," Simon says. He points both hands down at the orb. "I've finally been able to hold the portal open. I have the boys down in research analyzing the energy patterns."

A crooked smile makes its way across Geno's face.

"I'll go ahead and get some men for the portal," Geno responds. Simon quickly looks up.

"Wait, no," he begins in a stern tone. "We can't send ANY men to get close to it yet. We aren't sure how safe it is. We need to perform tests with animals or objects."

"Simon, I am the leader of this operation," Geno states. He leans over the screen. "We will do what I decide. The CDD takes pride in being a leading innovator, but we need something for me to go public."

"What is it with you, Geno?" Simon yells out. His neck turns a soft tomato color. "Why can't you just go public as the head of the CDD? Hell, I've had to say I built this place from the ground up the whole time."

"It's not important, Simon," Geno responds. His form stays straight and his voice remains stoic. "What is important is the task we are facing."

"I refuse to send innocent men to their deaths," Simon calls out. "I refuse to put lives at risk like this. You're a selfish goddamn bastard."

"SELFISH?" Geno cries out in anger. He slams his fists down onto the screen, which causes a few small cracks to form. Veins bulge from his neck and he turns his face up. The light shines upon his pink skin and his bloodshot eyes pulse. "What I am doing is not SELFISH!"

Simon takes a few steps back as Geno steadily stomps around the screen. Simon backs up into a desk, bumping into a computer which switches the screen on. An image of one of the scientists with their wife and two children appears, which lights up Geno as he walks out of the light.

"We could save MILLIONS of people," Geno yells out. He stabs his finger into Simon's chest, and digs around. "We could take the materials and resources to further our research and to further our world. If we have to sacrifice a few to save a million, why not?"

"You're sick Geno," Simon says through clenched teeth. "You need help."

"No," Geno says in a calmer, yet more serious tone. He pulls his finger out and regains his composure. "What I need is for you to do as I fucking say."

"I'm your partner, Geno," Simon responds. He covers the hole in his chest with his hands. "Decisions need to be made between us."

"Then maybe," Geno begins. "I need to send you in there myself."

Simon's eyes widen. Geno turns and walks back to the screen, where he enlarges the video and pushes down on an intercom button. Simon takes the opportunity to open up an application on the computer behind him.

"I would like all personnel to report to the meeting room where we will commence our operation," Geno speaks into the speaker next to the screen. Simon opens up a console where he clicks in some code and the keyboard's loudness alerts Geno.

"Simon, what are you doing?" he asks. He walks

over to Simon, who tries to rush typing. Geno grabs onto his shoulder and throws him away from the computer. Simon slides across the floor and slams into the far wall. A painting of Martin Geno falls. Geno leans over the computer and reads the code. "Trying to close the portal, are you?"

"I can't risk the lives of anyone," Simon says as he pulls himself up. "It's not worth it."

Geno sighs and steps away from the computer. He slightly hunches over as he walks over to Simon, and reaches an arm of help out.

"I guess you are right," Geno says. Simon hesitates before grabbing onto Geno's hand, and he's thrusted up. As Simon rises, Geno plunges his fist right through Simon's stomach. "But I can risk whatever I want in the name of science."

Simon gasps for air as Geno's fist wiggles around his intestines. Blood pools from his mouth and stains his suit. Geno pats Simon's back and slowly removes his fist. Geno holds up Simon's body by his collar, and pats his head.

"The suit you'll wear will heal the unfortunate hole I gave you," Geno laughs. "And I hope you find something good on the other side. Because once you're gone from the public eye, and I know for a fact you are dead, I am going to reveal my part in everything. And you will be wiped from history."

Simon's vision fades and he passes out, and Geno's

face is the last thing he sees.

———

"And that's how I ended up here," Simon tells the rest of the group. "And then I met Barney and you two."

"Twenty years alone, what did you do?" Janus asks. Simon walks over to him and places a hand on his shoulder. Janus gives him a weird look.

"I did what scientists do and I researched this world," Simon explains. "And I believe that if someone enters this world, this place creates a copy of them and then they stumble into our world. Or maybe even other worlds."

"So, how can we figure out who's a-," Janus begins, but is interrupted by a knock on the door. Everyone stands still and remains quiet. They stare at the door, seeing a shadow of two feet pour from underneath. Simon looks at the other three and slowly raises a finger to his mouth. He takes a step toward the door, and Barney mouths him to stop. As Simon gets closer to the knob, Janus' head spikes with pain. He covers his mouth to muffle the scream he lets out, and almost falls to the ground.

"Don't open the door!" Barney whispers loudly. Simon moves his head back as he carefully turns the knob open. He lets go, and the door is pushed open by whomever is on the other side. Simon steps back, and as the door opens, he looks back at Janus, who is now on the ground convulsing.

"You killed my mother!" the figure in the door yells as he pounces onto Simon, who lets out a yell as he falls to the ground. The figure is cast in shadow as the lights suddenly shut off, and a voice calls over from the loudspeakers.

"INTRUDER ALERT! INTRUDER ALERT!" a calm, robotic voice calls from the speakers. The noise echoes through the halls outside, and the sound of marching grows louder. Barney runs over to Janus and tries to hold his shaking body still. Simon is held down by the figure as he pulls out a sharpened bark and shoves it into Simon's shoulder blade. He yells out in pain as the figure twists and turns the embedded stick. Marcus leans over and leaps forward, knocking the figure to the ground next to Simon. Marcus looks down to see the figure's face, as red emergency lights begin to flash outside.

The face is illuminated for seconds at a time, and it looks like a beaten Janus. Marcus looks over to Janus who continues to thrash around. Marucs puts two and two together and slaps Janus Wrench right across the face, and pulls him up by his overall's straps. Marcus throws Janus Wrench into the wall, and blood splatters across the room.

"Barney!" Marcus yells out over the siren noise that accompanies the loudspeaker message. "Get Janus out of here!"

"What about Simon?" Barney yells out, hoisting Janus over his shoulder. He stands up and runs over to the open door, looking down the halls for signs of guards.

"Just get Janus out of here, and I'll handle this," Marcus says. Barney nods and he runs to the right with Janus over his shoulder. Marcus turns around and faces Janus Wrench, who stands in the red light. Simon crawls up the wall to his feet, and he removes the piece of bark from his back.

"Are you ok?" Marcus asks Simon, while staring at Janus Wrench. Simon nods as he manually breathes.

"Yeah, I should be fine," he responds. "Do we run? Or fight?"

"We run," Marcus answers. Simon nods and they both run out of the door at the same time. Due to their size, they both get caught in the door together, but they're able to squeeze through. They both fall to the ground, but they scramble up and run down the right side of the hall. The wooden walls bleed red as the emergency lights flash on and off. The marching noises grow louder behind them, and Marcus looks back to see a battalion of armed guards running full speed at them.

They turn a corner, and run into a large white testing room. Along both sides of the room are medical tubes with bodies floating in greenish-yellow liquids. A few scientists jump out of the way as Marcus and Simon push through them. Simon runs past a rack of vials and test tubes right next to the double exit doors, and he throws it to the ground, which blocks the path and causes liquids and goo to spill across the floor. The guards try to jump over, but a few fall face-first into the mixture.

Passing through the doors, Marcus and Simon run outside into a courtyard full of green bushes, and plentiful flower patches. They keep running without stopping, traveling the winding dirt paths that criss-cross between the gardens. A few yards away, they can spot a gated exit, and a running car on the other side. The window is cranked down, and Barney shoves his head out and yells to the two, who are unable to hear what he's saying.

"Is that Barney?" Marcus yells as he struggles for breath. The two are both not good runners, as their size limits them.

"I hope so, because if that's Geno than we are fucked," Simon responds. In the car, Barney looks at the backseat to see Janus resting peacefully. The car is a custom-made black Humvee M1123, with armor plates on the outside, a turret on top, and heavy-duty wheels. As Marcus and Simon reach the gate, they notice its chained shut. Marcus pushes it as far as he can, and struggles to wiggle through. It rubs against his skin and tears a few sections of skin on his face. He gets his arm caught in the chain right as he reaches the other side.

"I'm stuck!" Marcus yells out. Simon looks at the chain to see it wrapped around Marcus' arm. He hears running and screaming from the CDD, and turns back to see guards running through the garden. "Simon, let's go!"

"No, I have a plan," Simon quickly says. He grabs onto Marcus' hand and pushes it out of the tangled chains. Marcus falls to the ground, rolling a few feet to Barney's car. "Get in the car, and hide. I'll come back."

"We can't just leave you!" Marcus yells out as he stands up next to the vehicle. Simon laughs.

"Yes you can," he responds. The guards catch up to Simon, beating him to the ground and dragging his bleeding body back to the CDD. His blood smears along the dirt path as the guards slam their batons down onto his flabby body. Marcus watches as he jumps into the passenger seat of the car, and some guards stare at him as they drive away. They drive into the forest, finding somewhere to hide as Marcus and Barney discuss a plan to break back in.

10

S.O.S.

"How are you doing?"

Janus opens his eyes to see Marcus sitting in the passenger seat, turned around to look at him. Janus sits up on the black leather seats, and looks out the windows through squinted eyes. The sight of trees passes by, and all the green and colorful nature shines under the sun, which is being revealed by the clouds. Janus leans forward to see Barney driving, and he keeps one hand on the gear shift as he does.

"I'm fine," Janus says. "My head feels better than last time."

Through the front window, Janus sees the CDD through the tree line, and the proximity gate coming up fast. Marcus raises a fist toward Janus, who takes a moment to realize, and gives him a fist bump.

"Why are we going back?" Janus asks. "And where's Simon?"

"Simon is right," Barney says, pointing two fingers out of the window. "There."

"In the CDD?" Janus worryingly exclaims. "How

did we escape, but he didn't?"

"He let himself get captured, that crazy bastard," Marcus answers. "And besides, we needed to get you healed."

"Why?" Janus asks. Marcus taps his leg, and Janus pulls up his pant leg. Across his skin are stitched up cuts and blood-stained surgical tape wrapped all around. "What happened?"

"We had a bumpy exit," Barney says. "But you're all good, no life-threatening wounds. That I know of."

"There's no hospitals around?" Janus asks.

"Dude, there's barely ANYONE around," Marcus responds. "The only medical personnel in the area are in that building, probably operating or torturing Simon."

"What are we going to do now?" Janus asks. "Waltz back in and ask for Simon back? We'll be dead on arrival."

"Well, I have been thinking of an idea," Marcus says. "And I have one."

"Oh god," Janus says.

"Uh oh," Barney sighs.

"We ask them for help," Marcus exclaims in an exciting tone, keeping his mouth open in excitement as he waits for a reaction. Janus and Barney exchange a glance through the rearview mirror. "What?"

"The CDD?" Janus says. "For help?"

"Yes, we just disguise ourselves and ask for help," Marcus responds. "Foolproof plan. Absolutely nothing can go wrong."

"They are going to kill us," Barney says, putting his other hand on the wheel. "Once they know we're the ones helping Simon, we're dead. BEFORE arrival."

"It's the only thing we have," Marcus says to Barney. Barney shakes his head.

"It's risky, man," he responds. "I don't think it's worth it."

"It might be risky," Marcus says. "But what else can we do?"

"I guess you're right," Barney groans. "But how are we going to get disguises?"

—

A CDD guard stands outside the front sliding door. He stands up straight with his gun cradled in his arm, like a King's Guard. He watches the front lawn and arrival area with a cold stare, watching for any movement. He sees a singular man emerge from the tree line outside the gate. The guard squints his eyes and furrows his brow, walking down the steep hill to the gate's entrance.

The person on the other side is a large man wearing clothes made of leaves held together by tree sap. A millipede corpse sticks to his top lip, resembling a handlebar mustache. The man's hair is sticking straight up, and pokes out in different directions, like a naval mine. He stands with his legs out, and his feet pointing inward.

"Hello," the man says, with a bubbly and stuffy voice. The guard stares on in confusion. "Is this the

CDD?"

"Who are you?" the guard scolds in a deep and overbearing voice. "State your business."

"Oh! MY name is Semen Cold!" the man responds. He raises his arms in excitement and a few leaves fall down. "And my friend is in danger!"

He grabs onto the bars on the gate, pulling them back and forth. The guard jumps back and raises his gun toward the man, who jumps back in fear.

"Get back!" he yells out, his dark skin bulging with veins.

"Please, sir!" the man cries out. "Our friend! Is dying!"

"Stay back, you doppelganger fucks!" the guard yells, keeping his aim on the man's head. The man holds his hands up in defense.

"Doppelgangers?" he asks. "No, no, no! I am not a doppelganger, I am a man! Like you!"

From the tree line, Janus and Barney watch on in absolute shock. They watch as Marcus dances around like a complete buffoon, all while the guard is trying to threaten him away. Janus shakes his head and Barney slams his palm on his forehead.

"I'm going out there," Janus says. He stands up from his crouching position, but Barney grabs his shoulder and pulls him back down.

"Are you crazy?" Barney yells quietly. "There's a guy with a gun over there!"

"I've dealt with worse," Janus laughs. He stands up, but Barney pulls him down again. "What, dude?"

"Janus!" Barney says. "We should just turn back now, and-"

Barney turns to look around the forest for the car, but it's gone. He gasps and hears footsteps behind him, and when he turns again he sees Janus booking it toward Marcus.

"...need to get out of here," the guard says. He sees Janus in the corner of his eye and takes a step back. "Who is that?"

The dancing man looks at Janus, shrugging when he turns back to the guard.

"MARCUS!" Janus yells out. "TELL HIM ABOUT SIMON!"

The guard's eyes open.

"Simon?" he asks. "You need to see Simon Wrench?"

"YES!" Janus cries out as his feet slap against the dirt path. He runs up next to the mysterious man, who takes a step away. Janus grabs onto the bars and through gasping breath he continues to speak. "SIMON! WRENCH! WE NEED! TO SEE! HIM!"

"Jesus, alright," the guard reluctantly says. He looks back to the man. "You stay."

"No, he's with us," Barney says as he leisurely reaches Janus.

"Who are you guys?" the man asks. From the trees,

Marcus walks out with a beehive on his head. He runs around in circles screaming, bees flying around his body and stinging him all over.

"If Marcus is down there," Janus says. "Than who the fuck are you?"

"Semen Cold," the man responds with a disgusted face. "I'm here with my friends Jank Feeterson and Barnyard. Jank has a rectal infection, and his anus is protruding from his mouth."

"Ok, what the fuck, shut the fuck up," Barney says grabbing onto his stomach and turning green. The guard takes a thing of keys off his belt, unlocking the gate. Janus runs over to Marcus quickly, removing the beehive and throwing it away.

"Oh, hey Janus!" he says through a swollen mouth. His entire face is just red bubbles. Janus grabs his enlarged arm, pulling him toward the CDD. Marcus waddles as he runs, bouncing on both of his swollen legs. The guard lets the three through, locking the gate on Semen's face. He walks the trio up to the front lobby, and activates his walkie.

"Hey, I'm letting three guys inside," he says. "They need to see Simon Wrench, and they aren't doppelgangers. I've checked them out."

"Copy that," a voice responds from the walkie. The front sliding doors open, and the trio walks in.

"Good luck," the guard says to them as the door closes behind. The trio looks around at the empty golden-trimmed lobby. Across the room on the far wall, a large map of the building hangs above a purple leather couch. The trio walks over, looking at the abstract floor plan.

"Are you here for ze Simon Wrench?" a German-sounding doctor asks, walking out of a door on their right. He wears a stained white apron, blue surgical gloves, a surgical mask, and large steampunk-esque goggles. "He is alive…and very well."

11

Crisis Averted

Simon sits still, bound by rope to a metal folding chair. A glued blindfold covers his eyes.

"Hello?" he asks, hoping someone else is there with him.

"You aren't supposed to be speaking," a commanding voice booms. "You're a prisoner, and prisoners aren't granted rights."

"We can probably work something out," Simon says back. "Seems you have anger issues, maybe we can talk about your feelings?"

The man rips the blindfold from Simon's face, pulling some patches of skin off. Blood drips out. Simon groans from the sudden sharp pain, and looks up at the melted guard staring at him. The guard's face is all melted and greasy, like pulled-pork. It's been put back in place and kept up by nails driven deep into his skin. His eyes are hidden by drooping bloody eyelids, and his mouth is perpetually stuck in a smile. His uniform is covered in blood, sweat stains, and flies.

"I could buy you a toothbrush?" Simon says,

turning his head away as the guard slaps him across his face. "Or not."

"You stay here, I need to check something," the guard says, spit flying onto Simon's bruised cheek. He turns around and walks through the empty, white-padded room and opens the door to the hallway outside. Before he can close it behind him, a walkie-talkie on his belt switches on.

"Liquelle," Geno's voice comes through. The guard takes the walkie off his waist and up to his mouth.

"Yes, boss?" he asks.

"Progress report."

"Mr. Geno, we have Simon Wrench alive and well," Liquelle answers. He looks back at Simon for a moment. "He's normal and has no signs of infection."

"Thank you for letting me know," Geno sighs. "Make sure Dr. Mengele gets his tools before he extracts Simon's energy."

"Yes, sir," Liquelle responds.

"And if you see Ron," Geno continues. "Make sure he knows to come to my office the moment he can."

Liquelle shuts the door, and the white light above Simon cuts out, and the smell of burnt meat fills the room.

—

Geno stands next to his table. Scientists work at their computers around the room. The lights are all on, and the room is illuminated. The black walls reflect no light at all, and the stained carpet grows mushrooms from the light. A CDD guard runs in, and hands Geno a folded piece of paper. Geno opens it, and a CCTV photo shows Ron with the fugitives entering the CDD.

"So, he's with them now?" Geno asks.

"We think he's bringing them to you," the guard responds. "They're trying to see Simon."

"Is the portal on?" Geno asks, crushing the photo in his hand and letting it fall to the ground.

"No, sir," the guard answers. "We shut it off when they were spotted outside."

"Good."

"When is Simon's operation?" the guard asks.

"Now."

—

Simon is wheeled out in a rusty wheelchair down grimy halls and past trashed surgical equipment and wandering patients. He struggles to keep his eyes open, and his vision is completely blurred. An IV is stuck in his arm, hastily taped down. The left wheel is broken, and the wheelchair occasionally jumps up. Dr. Mengele wheels him down the halls, avoiding the overturned hospital beds and overdosing patients, pushing through the double doors into the surgery room. Simon phases in and out of consciousness as he passes out, and wakes up a few moments later.

His nose activates first, smelling the rot and dirt around him. His ears are next, hearing the hum of an A/C machine and the grinding of medical tools. He blinks his eyes open, and looks up at the broken tiled ceiling. Shattered lights look down on him like dark eyes. Simon turns his head to the right, where he sees a man bend over a moldy sink. He washes some bloody tools under brown water. He wears only a bloody white apron, with his aged and wrinkled skin out for the wind to kiss.

"Mr. Simon, you are a hard one to catch," the man says. He turns the water off and lays the wet tools on a metal plate. Simon looks around the rest of the room, where he finds himself nailed down to a wooden plank, with lights and an IV around the left side of the room. Around the walls, medical degrees and counters covered in bloody tissues and sticky tissues fill the space. The man turns around and Simon looks at his face.

His face droops naturally, and his thick black eyebrows hang over his wide eyes. He dons a fake smile, with a noticeable gap between his front two teeth. His hair is dark and combed over, with a nice split line on the left side. His face is aged and wrinkled, with bumps and holes across the skin.

"Who are you?" Simon asks. The doctor laughs.

"I am Dr. Josef Rudolf Mengele," the German doctor responds. His accent is thick and recognizable. "I am not a doppelganger of ze once great man. I was believed to have…drowned, off ze coast of Bertioga. However, I was transported here, and began to study ze world."

"You're the Nazi doctor?" Simon yells out. The

doctor laughs once more. He picks up the metal plate and brings it over to a small table next to Simon. Simon looks down at the horrid, jagged tools that still have the brown water on them.

"The Nazi party was once a great one, however," Dr. Mengele begins. "All good things must come to an end."

"What are you going to do to me?" Simon asks. Dr. Mengele lifts up his surgical mask, and pulls a machine out from under the plank. Simon is unable to see it, since he can't move his head. The doctor lifts up a breathing apparatus, placing it on Simon's mouth. Simon thrashes around, trying to move his face out of the way, but the doctor grabs his head and keeps it still. Simon stares at the doctor with horror as he places the apparatus on his mouth. Simon stops as he breathes in the anesthesia.

"Goodnight, Mr. Wrench," the doctor says, as Simon falls asleep.

—

Simon awakes completely numb, and back in the wheelchair. He's in the lobby of the surgical wing, where rows of empty chairs rot and rust away. A hum of lights fills the room, and the smells are the same as in the surgery room itself. He opens his eyes slowly, and sees Geno and Dr. Mengele through blurry vision. They have their backs turned to Simon, and discuss something loudly. The IV in Simon's arm pumps him with his own blood.

"We have a new shipment of S-12," Geno says.

83

"Can you merge it with Simon's sample?"

"Yes, of course," Dr. Mengele responds. "We can get Dr. Peterson on it."

"Once we find a way to combat the S-12, we can begin Project: Worlds Collide," Geno whispers. Simon is still able to hear them. "We can't risk the planet being corrupted without a cure. If we have a way to fix it, they will pay us big time."

"Of course, sir," Dr. Mengele nods. "I will bring Simon out to the others, and we can speak with Dr. Peterson."

"Good work," Geno says. He pats Dr. Mengele on the shoulder, and walks out of the squeaky double doors. Dr. Mengele turns around, and Simon passes out once more.

12

Zombies!

anus, Marcus, and Barney wait on a rusty metal bench. They sit before the medical wing entrance, in a small room home to a few beeping computers, portraits of unnamed people, and a lack of any sort of life beside the trio. Janus waits eagerly for Simon, tapping his feet and humming a tune. Marcus has his arms crossed and is completely knocked out. Barney is staring right at a painting across the room from him. In between a few landscapes and abstract pieces, a single framed oil painting of a brown and tan mixed cat hanging from a branch catches his eye. He feels as though the painting is speaking to him.

The room smells of alcohol, medical wipes, and plastic wrap. The air feels dirty and wet, which matches the moist, squishy walls. The bench is jagged in some places, and it's covered in a layer of dust.

"Barney," Janus says. Barney snaps from his concentration.

"Yeah?" Barney asks. He crosses his arms and leans back.

"Have you noticed that a lot of houses look the

same on the outside?"

"I'm homeless," Barney says.

"Right," Janus says. "I think designers are getting lazier."

"What are you two talking about?" Marcus asks, sitting up and opening his eyes. "About houses?"

"Just some small talk," Janus responds. "It's been a while. I wonder what he's getting surgery for."

"The doctor didn't tell us much," Barney says, looking to his right, right at a small desk. Behind it is a large-scale black and white portrait of the doctor wearing a high-collared suit and hat. Atop his hat is a medallion of an eagle, and on the right side of his collar is a double S logo. His stare perpetually watches the room.

"Be patient," Marcus says. "It's gonna take time."

"The doctor didn't tell us what Simon was getting." Janus stands up, walking over to the desk, where a disorganized pile of papers are spread over it. He flips through a few, with each one showcasing different people marked as 'SUBJECTS.' Janus finds one with Simon's name on it from 1978, but is stopped when the double doors open. He quickly walks in front of the desk, dropping the file in the process. Dr. Mengele pushes Simon on the wheelchair out, and stops him in the middle of the room.

"He is done with his operation," Dr. Mengele says. "He will not be able to do any sort of physical activity, or-"

"It looks like he hasn't done anything too physical

86

in a while," Barney cuts in laughing. Dr. Mengele looks at him with a dead stare. "Sorry."

"I hope you all have a great day, and I wish you all the best of luck," Dr. Mengele says before walking backward through the doors into the room beyond. Janus rushes over to Simon, who sits on the wheelchair passed out. He wears a white hospital gown, with his black suit folded over his legs. His skin is pale and his hair is greasy. He looks horrible, like someone who was just shot to the point of death.

"Simon?" Janus asks. He holds up Simon's head, but it feels cold to the touch. An alarm sound suddenly erupts in the room, and a red light spins on the wall. "What the hell?"

Screaming comes from the other side of the door, and the doors burst open with a CDD scientist missing a head. Blood squirts from the wound, and covers Janus completely. He spits out some blood and wipes it from his eyes. The walkie on Barney's belt switches on.

"A DOPPELGANGER-," a voice comes through. "A GROUP OF DOPPELGANGERS BROKE IN."

"I...," Simon whispers. "Get the IV...out."

Janus quickly grabs onto the IV in Simon's arm, pulling it out. The color flushes back to Simon's skin, and he coughs up some blood, although it has a purple hue.

"I...know how to get out," Simon says, his voice louder than before. He points at the door the trio were brought from by Dr. Mengele. Barney runs to the door as

Marcus grabs onto the wheelchair handles. Barney pushes open the door as Semen Cold pounces from the other side. He looks almost the same from before, but his skin is flared with purple lines and crumbling black rock-like patches.

"HELP!" Barney yells out as Semen slashes at his face with long fingernails. Marcus runs past the others, kicking Semen in his stomach. Marcus' foot goes right through Semen's chest, and Semen is split in half. His legs fall to the ground next to Barney, but his upper half launches into the ceiling. Marcus feels something slither into his shoe, but doesn't pay too much mind to it. He runs back to Simon, and pushes him out of the room.

"We can leave through the vents," Simon says, trying to stand from the wheelchair. They turn the corner down the hallway where the reception desk is, but a group of guard corpses line the walls. A few limbless doppelgangers consume the bodies of the dead, with clouds of purple around them. "Ok, not the vents."

A guard runs out from the reception room, flailing his arms and running toward the group.

"Don't go to the basement!" he yells out. "There's a whole group of them!"

"The basement is a no-go, then," Simon says. "There's a back door somewhere. It leads to the outside."

"Wait," Marcus cuts in. "How do you NOT know where it is? Isn't this your place?"

"I...can't remember," Simon says, looking down at

his hands. He pushes himself forward off the wheelchair, nearly falling onto the ground. His legs wobble as he holds himself up. "We just need to get away."

"I agree," Janus, Marcus, and Barney all say in unison.

"Look," Marcus begins. "There's so many doppelgangers everywhere. We may need to split up."

"Split up?" Janus screams. "Are you insane?"

"You have any other idea?" Barney asks. Janus holds up the middle finger at him.

"Splitting up is what they do in horror movies!" Janus says.

"It's the only thing we can do," Marcus shrugs. "Barney and I will go through the medical wing, and you and Simon can go...the other way."

"We can get a walkie off the headless guard," Simon says. Janus shakes his head and walks past the wheelchair, kicking it over as he does. It falls to the ground with a metallic clank. Simon looks back at Marcus and Barney.

"Stay safe," he says to Marcus who flashes him a quick smile.

"You too."

13

Barney and Marcus

arney and Marcus walk the endless, looping CDD hallways. They have traveled to the medical wing, where the grimy white walls, greasy floors, and wandering zombie-like patients scream health violation.

Hunched-back, skeletal figures stumble around the cluttered halls and rooms, cast in shadow from the dim or broken fluorescent lights. Boils and bubbles dot their stretched skin, and blood stains their white gowns. They groan as they walk, and their bones crack and shake.

"You see Simon yet?" Barney asks Marcus. He looks down each hall, door, and through every little window or crack. Marcus doesn't respond, and he walks with his head down. "Marcus?"

"What?" Marcus says, snapping out of a trance. They pass by an overturned hospital bed, and a charred body lies next to it. Marcus steps over the black and orange skull.

"Have you seen any signs of the exit? Or even Geno?" Barney asks once more. Marcus shakes his head.

"No."

"You alright?" Barney asks. He stops looking around for a moment and holds his hand out in front of Marcus. "You good?"

Marcus is covered in sweat, and his eyelids droop down. His eyes are devoid of color, and his skin is as pale as it can get. Marcus takes a seat behind him on a rusty waiting bench, right outside a set of double doors. A sign extending out above it reads 'SURGERY.'

"Yeah," Marcus responds. He places a hand on his forehead and closes his eyes. "I just need to rest."

A soft glow emits from his sleeve as he puts his hand up.

"Hey, what's that?" Barney asks. He reaches over to Marcus' sleeve and pulls it down. Marcus tries to swat his hand away, but is too late. Barney reveals Marcus' arm, which is covered in dark purple cracks and rocks. His skin is slowly crumbling away, and a few pieces drop off onto the ground. Marcus sighs and looks away, putting his sleeve back up. The glow is concealed.

"You're infected," Barney says, taking a seat next to Marcus.

"It's alright," Marcus responds. Barney thinks for a second.

"I've…seen it before," he explains. "The infection is not safe. You won't make it at this rate."

"That's alright," Marcus responds. He rests his arms on his legs and lays his head back. He breathes from his mouth, and Barney can see a few rocks fall from his nose. "It's ok."

"We can try to save you," Barney says. "The others, they-"

"Don't tell the others," Marcus cuts Barney off. He closes his eyes.

"They need to know, Marcus," Barney says. Marcus doesn't respond. "What about Janus?"

"Janus can't know," Marcus finally says after a full minute of silence between the two of them. "I'm all he has...if he finds out...he'll be destroyed."

"He's going to find out one way or another," Barney responds. Marcus nods. "We can give you to the scientists here, and you can be operated on."

"No," Marcus says. "No."

"Why not?"

"Geno will find us and kill Simon."

"What if he doesn't?" Barney asks.

"What if he does?"

Marcus opens his monochrome eyes and looks at Barney. Barney looks away.

"He's not to be trusted, Barney."

"No one is to be trusted."

"Simon is," Marcus says. A few patients roam the halls around them, falling over trash and puking on the walls.

"Marcus," Barney says. "I won't tell Janus. But you will die sooner than later."

"I just need to get Janus and Simon to our world

again," Marcus says. He closes his eyes and looks away again. He takes a deep breath and stands up, stretching his back and taking a few steps away. "I think we better get going."

"I think so, too," Barney responds. He gets up and follows behind Marcus. They both walk down the hallway, passing by the surgery room as a shadowy figure in the frosted glass of the doors looks out, red eyes glowing through.

14

Martin Geno Enters

"Sir, are you sure you want to do this?" a guard asks Martin Geno, who stands before the CDD doppel barrier. It's located in a room located in the bottom-most level of the building, and allows anyone to cross into the doppelganger world at any point. Geno has crossed over a few times, but now he is going to stay for a longer amount of time.

"I've most likely grown immune to the effects," Geno responds. He stands in a blank room, with rebar and metal supports holding up the entirety of the CDD. The barrier takes the form of blue streaks, which beckon Geno forward with sounds of encouragement.

"Sir, the longest you've stayed in the doppel world was twenty-four hours," the guard says. "You were on a limit that took you out when you reached that time."

"And I'm saying I don't want the stupid goddamn limit anymore," Geno yells at the guard, who stands in the far left corner at a little station with a control panel. He wears a blue hard hat and a light gray uniform that matches the unpainted room. "But I need that cure. If one of those creatures bites me, I'm not letting myself die."

"Yes, sir," the guard shakingly responds. He walks over to Geno, and hands him a black walkie-talkie, and a small metal flask. Geno puts both into the inside pockets of his suit jacket. "You can enter whenever you are ready."

"You don't need to tell me when to go," Geno states. He pushes the guard back, and steps forward, breaking through the barrier. He feels the streaks of blue swirl around him, pulling him along as he travels across universes in one single step. As his other foot comes down on the ground of the doppel world, he feels the gravitational pull and air quality change like a snap of his fingers.

"Hello? Can you hear me?" a glitchy voice calls out from the walkie-talkie. Geno pulls it out of his pocket and holds his thumb down.

"I'm here, yes," Geno says. He wanders around the empty room, walking into the exit elevator, which takes him up to the CDD lobby. He steps out into the polished gold-furnished chamber, with expensive velvet chairs and a million-dollar piano huddle in the corner. Paintings of Martin Geno and his lineage before him adorn the walls, and a carpet sewn by Geno's great, great grandmother lines the floor. The CDD is the same place in both worlds, and some scientists travel from Geno's world to the doppel world for tests. A few scientists and guards populate the lobby, and they all bow as Geno walks past. He walks across the shining lobby, out of the sliding glass doors, and into the doppel world's forest.

"You should be in a forest," the guard says from the walkie. Geno confirms with a ten-four. He walks through some of the tree paths, looking around for signs of criminal activity. As he explores, a crack in the distance alerts him. He quickly hides behind one of the trees, looking down a dirt path to see a figure wandering around and holding the side of his face.

"Someone is here," Geno tells the guard. He turns the walkie's volume down as he slowly approaches the figure. "Who's there!"

The figure hears his voice, and violently turns its back almost all the way around, staring at Geno as he takes one step at a time. The figure hunches over and watches Geno like a bird.

"You look familiar," Geno says softly. He reaches a hand out, which the figure watches closely. "Could you be lost, friend?"

"It's you…," the figure says. He lowers his hand from his face, and a large chunk of flesh is revealed to be missing. "From the lab. Geno?"

"Ah, Simon's boy," Geno responds. He knows the boy as Janus Wrench, Simon's only child. Geno conducted experiments on the boy after Simon and Mary's disappearances. Geno took him in as his own for years, torturing and mutilating him all to further science. "I almost didn't recognize you. Here, come, and I'll take you to shelter."

"I need my father," Janus cries out. "I feel him

here…with me."

"Oh, you poor soul," Geno lies. "He's here with me, waiting for you. I can take you with me, if you'd like?"

"Please…I'm so lost. So alone," Janus says. "I don't know where I am, and I have flashes where I'm not myself and something takes control over me."

"I'm on my way to see him now, so come with me," Geno says, reaching his hand out farther. Janus steps forward, touching his hand with his blood-stained fingers. Geno gently pulls him forward, pointing toward the CDD. "That is where your father is."

"I don't even remember what he looks like," Janus says. He looks down to his feet, which are scarred from walking across splintering wood. Geno smiles at Janus.

"Come with me, and you'll remember."

—

- April 4th, 1982 -

Beep.

Beep.

Beep.

"The two people in this picture look exactly alike."

Beep.

"We found both of these boys in the woods."

Beep.

"What we did was combine the boys into one full, organic being…"

Beep.

"And then we found another boy that matches their DNA."

Beep.

"And we combined him into Subject C-2."

"Good," a second voice cuts in. The voices are drastically different, with one proper and firm, and the other nerdy and fast-paced. Janus Wrench opens his eyes, and Martin Geno stands over him. A bright white light shines on behind him. A doctor with a farmer's tan on his head, thick circular glasses, and a goatee stands on Janus' right holding a clipboard and looking at a heart rate monitor.

Janus looks around at the white-padded room, freshly cleaned and claustrophobic. He's tied to a medical bed, and a golden mask covers his face. He tries to speak, but the disguise holds his lips shut. Geno dons his usual black suit, and he takes a photo from the scientist.

"And you have found another?" Geno asks.

"Yes, and we have his essence trapped in a needle," the scientist nods. "Before, we'd combine them using a machine but we have since found a way to use this golden mask to inject him with the DNA of the clones."

"We call them doppelgangers, Dr. Spitelle," Geno says, pointing a finger at the scientist. "But you may start with the procedure."

"Yes, sir," Dr. Spitelle responds. Geno walks out of the room, and Dr. Spitelle places his clipboard down onto a rolling table. He picks up a needle filled with glowing lime liquid, and he flicks the top. "Stay still, son."

Janus watches as Dr. Spitelle leans over his body and lowers the needle into his eye. Janus thrashes around on the bed as Dr. Spitelle tries to inject the needle. He holds down Janus with his arms and grabs onto his neck.

"Hold still, you little fucker!" Dr. Spitelle yells out at the twelve-year old boy. Geno watches from his little observation room. His expression is stoic, knowing that everything he does is in the name of science. He has no remorse for the son of his former colleague. He has no remorse for anyone.

15

A Way Out?

"You remind me of my son."

"What?" Janus asks.

"My son," Simon says again. They walk through the clean white halls of the testing halls. Colorful lines on the ground lead to certain rooms and chambers, and frosted windows across the walls block people from looking in. Simon and Janus walk and talk, looking out for the exit. No guards or anyone patrol the halls, so they freely move about.

"My son, whom I named Janus, like your name, looks just like you," Simon says, smiling from the memories. "I haven't seen him in so long. He was just a child when I disappeared…I hope he's still out there in our world."

"I know we'll find a way out," Janus assures him. "We have had good luck so far."

They turn a corner, which ends almost immediately. The wall ends and is covered with different posters and pictures. However, through a small hole in the collage, Simon sees his own face. He scratches his head and tears down the advertisements, revealing a mirror behind it.

They look at themselves, admiring their clean looks, until they both realize a figure stands behind them. They slowly turn around to see Dr. Mengele from earlier towering above them. He wears a German Mardi Gras mask, which looks like a disgruntled old clown.

"Hello, boys, I've been looking for you," he says through the mask. He places a hand on their shoulders, leaning over to make eye contact. His grip tightens on their shoulders, to which Simon and Janus look at eachother and gulp. "Guests are not permitted in the lower wings."

On Simon's belt, his walkie-talkie switches on. Barney's voice comes through.

"Simon!" he yells out. "We found the exit! It's on the South side of the building, near the medical wing."

"Looks like we have to go!" Simon says to Dr. Mengele. He tries to break free of the doctor's grip, but it's too strong. The doctor slowly turns his head to stare at Simon, who tries to move backward. The sound of marching echoes through the halls, which distracts Dr. Mengele, who loosens his hands. Janus and Simon both let themselves fall to the ground, breaking free from the doctor. He looks down as Simon and Janus crawl to their feet, running down the hall past a battalion of guards.

"Dr. Mengele, sir!" the leader says. He stomps his foot down as he stops, saluting the doctor with an outstretched right arm. The doctor storms up to the leader.

"Are you blind?" the doctor screams in a high pitched voice. "You just ran past the intruders!"

"Oh, crap!" the leader cries to himself. "I'm so gonna get fired for this!"

He turns the group around and they march toward Janus and Simon, who have reached the medical wing. They weave between the debris around the grimy halls, knocking over drug addicts, doppelgangers, and elderly people until they push through a set of double doors leading to a stairwell. The steps are rusty metal, and half of them have already crumbled away. A ceiling window brings the sun's dull shine outside down with it. The walls are moist and brown, with dirt seeping across them.

Simon and Janus both look down the middle, over a loose railing. They see Barney and Marcus at the bottom, hiding beneath some boxes.

"We need to get down there," Janus whispers. He turns around and looks through the crack in the double doors, seeing the battalion marching through. They trample over the patients and medical supplies, jumping around like fruit flies. "Like now."

"Yeah, I know," Simon says. He quickly begins to run down the stairs, watching his feet to make sure he doesn't fall down the one-hundred and eight feet drop down the middle. He jumps over holes and loose steps, finally reaching the bottom as he hears the doors up top burst open. Janus follows quickly behind, and they both lift up the boxes to see Barney and Marcus covered in sweat. The bottom of the stairwell is cleaner than the medical wing, but covered in nature. Vines wrap around the stairs, and the exit door leads right into a back alley that's covered in yellow tall grass, drooping swamp trees, and assortments of flowers. Barney and Marcus jump as Janus and Simon reveal them.

"Where's the exit at?" Simon asks.

"It's right in front of us," Marcus says, pointing to the rusting door frames that are woven with vines and tree roots. "But there's one problem."

"Yeah, and that's the guards trying to get us," Janus says. Marcus shakes his head with wide eyes.

"Not just that," he responds. "There's a doppelganger outside the door."

"So?" Simon asks.

"They're evolving," Marcus answers. "The doppelgangers are being corrupted now…and they're growing from it."

A purple glow from outside illuminates the mostly dark room, and the sound of guards above them echoes down. The glow grows stronger and stronger as a figure walks into view from the windowless frames. It's a skeleton with black bones and purple cracks all around it. He gives off a light hum and the smell of steak. He looks into the room with eyeless holes on his face and his jaw hanging open.

"Barney, you need to run out and distract him," Simon says. "Marcus and I are too fat-"

"Hey!" Marcus cries out.

"-and Janus is too skinny."

"Too skinny?" Janus asks himself.

"No," Barney says. He crawls back under the box. Simon lifts it up again.

"Yes. You need to go, and I'll find a car and pull it around."

Barney waits for a moment, and sees the doppelganger skeleton begin to crawl into the room. He looks up at Simon who nods and gives him a forced smile. Barney sighs and crawls out from the box, running past the doppelganger, which chases after him. Barney dives through the door frame, and the trio wait for a moment.

"Ok, it's time to go," Simon says. They slowly walk out of the room, hiding behind the doors as the guards fall down the stairs. They all pile up at the bottom of the room, and the leader falls on top of the pile.

"There's no one here!" he yells out. "I'm SO getting fired for this."

They all exit the pile and walk back up the stairs with their smiles gone and heads down. After the sound of their steps fades away, the trio stands up and runs through the forest. They find a nice abandoned golf cart sitting between two close trees. The leaves and grass around it have almost completely overtaken it. Simon pulls it from the ditch it made and searches around some bags on the cart for the keys. He digs through golf balls, golf clubs, and porno magazines before finally feeling the keys. He pulls out the silver metal, jumping into the driver's seat and slamming the key into the ignition.

"You all ready?" he asks, turning around to see Marcus and Janus slowly sit down on the back seat. They both nod as Simon turns the key, and the engine takes a few tries to finally switch on. Simon slams on the gas, almost hitting a tree, before circling the forest to find Barney up in a tree, with the doppelganger jumping up at him from underneath.

"SIMON!" Barney yells out, barely clinging to the branch. Simon squints his eyes, holding his foot over the gas as he slams into the doppelganger, which goes flying into a tree and shatters into a million bones. He brings the cart to a screeching halt under the tree, and lets Barney drop down. He climbs into the passenger seat, watching as the doppelganger's bones wiggle across the ground, combining together.

"I don't think we want to watch this," Janus says.

"Or be here for it," Marcus responds.

"Agreed," Simon says, as he turns the cart around the slams on the gas once more.

16

Reunited

"Good job, Barney," Simon says as he steers the golf cart through the trees. The dirt paths are bumpy, and the cart is never unmoving.

"Don't talk to me," Barney says, turning away from the others. Simon sighs.

"Come on, man," Simon says. "You're all good."

"I could've died," Barney complains.

"But you didn't!" Janus says from the backseat.

The sun above them shines through the green leaves above them.

"Let's…just go back to the house," Barney says.

The rest of the ride is set in silence, as none of the members want to talk. They all process the journey they just had escaping the CDD again. Janus picks at the skin on his fingers while Marcus catches a quick rest. Barney looks out into the tree line and Simon drives.

Eventually, they reach the house again. The chimney atop has fresh smoke billowing out. Simon is confused by this as he parks the cart at the bottom of the hill.

"Does anyone else see that?" Simon asks. Janus walks up next to him, looking up at the house.

"Nah, I see it too," he responds. Walking up to the door, Simon prepares himself for Geno on the other side. He reaches the wooden cabin door, to which he raises his fist and knocks three times. He stands straight for a few moments, as the door creaks open and a woman with curly brown hair is illuminated by the sun behind Simon. The woman steps out, and covers her mouth in shock.

"MARY?" Simon cries out. The woman nods her head, jumping up and giving Simon a large hug, squeezing his back. The woman is aged and a few gray hairs weave between the brown. Simon is suffering from the same as well. "Oh my god!"

"Simon! It can't be!" Mary exclaims, climbing down to her feet. "How did you get here? I thought you were dead!"

"It's me, Mary!" Simon yells in excitement. Marcus and Barney both climb the hill and catch up to them. "I've been here ever since nineteen-seventy-eight! This is where I went after I disappeared."

"What do you mean?" Mary asks. "How could you disappear and be sent…to Earth?"

"What?" Simon asks.

"You disappeared and have been here the whole time?" Mary asks.

"Yes."

"Why didn't you see me sooner?" Mary complains.

"Because…I didn't know you were on Earth-B too!"

"Earth-B?" Mary asks, to which Janus nods his head in agreement.

"That's the Earth we are on. This isn't our Earth, where our HOME home is," Simon explains. "This is a copy of our world, and a copy of our house."

"What?" Mary asks once more.

"You…didn't notice that nobody else is here?" Janus asks.

"I guess not," Mary says. "I haven't left the house much. Janus tells me not too, because I'll get sick. The only time I've been out recently is when we went to the woods to play hide and seek. Speaking of, where is Janus? And who are your friends?"

"Mary," Simon says, cutting Mary off. "He's gone. Not dead, but gone in terms of whereabouts. And we are lost to him and everyone else as well."

"Simon, you aren't making sense," Mary says. She takes a step backward into the house. "I'm not at home, but I am?"

"Yep," Marcus says. "By the way, we're Simon's friends and we're trying to all get the FUCK out of here."

"Yeah, Martin Geno is trying to kill us," Simon says.

"Geno?" Mary asks, putting a hand on her chest in disbelief. "Your little science buddy? Why would he ever want to do that?"

108

"I don't know," Simon responds. "But...is it possible if we could come in?"

"It's a lot to explain," Janus says.

"Of-of course," Mary says, stepping aside to let the four into the house. As she enters herself, she closes the door behind her as the sun sets, painting the sky orange and yellow.

—

- September 26th, 1978 -

Geno stands at a podium, before a large group of press and paparazzi. In front of him, a few dozen microphones are shoved into his face. The flashes of camera lights blind him for half of the speech. The rest of the town hall is obscured by banners of Martin Geno's company, and ones showcasing the portrait of Simon Wrench.

"SIR!" one of the reporters asks.

"Yes?" Geno says, trying to see who is getting his attention. He looks upon a young man, around twenty-two, who holds up a microphone to Geno's mouth.

"Who will run the company now that Simon Wrench is gone?" he asks. Geno smiles.

"I assure you, the CDD is in good hands," Geno says, holding up two thumbs up and looking around the room.

"Mr. Geno!" a reporter calls out. "How will you address the rumors of potential Russian and ex-Nazi communications?"

Geno's smile and cheerful demeanor fade.

"Mr. Geno!" another yells. "Is it true you are working with Kurt H. Debus on the Saturn V during the early seventies?"

"Mr. Geno! Are the rumors about you being the son of a Schutzstaffel officer?"

"How about…we cool it with all the Nazi talk, hm?" Geno yells out as sweat pours down his face. All of it is true, but he doesn't want to agree to any of it. He knows he is the son of Joseph Berchtold, in 1946, a year after being arrested. Joseph got it on with one of the female prison guards. Geno knows his heritage, and wears it proudly, yet secretly. Just a few months earlier, Geno was arrested on July 9th, in Chicago at a Nazi rally party.

"Mr. Geno!" one particular voice calls out. Geno looks through the moving crowd to see a singular, unmoving figure. As Geno tries to tell who he is, all goes black.

17

Goodbye, Friend

The group all sit at the table from earlier, as Mary comes into the room with a plate of drinks.

"Anyone want something?" she asks.

"What do you have?" Janus responds.

"Just some water, and some of Simon's leftover beer. It should still be good," Mary answers.

"We need to kill Martin Geno," Janus says through the conversation. "There's no way around it, it must be done."

"Hold on, we need to focus on escaping first," Marcus replies. Mary takes a seat next to the others. Barney leans over the table, taking a sip of his water.

"Kill a man?" Barney adds. "That's criminal."

"You don't understand him," Simon says. He crosses his arms and leans his head back over the chair. "He won't let anything but death stop him. He will keep doing experiments until he is DEAD."

"Well, how do you plan on killing him?" Marcus says as he loudly gulps down his drink. "We'll have no way home."

"There's no way that Geno is the only one that can control the barrier," Simon says. Barney groans.

"So," Barney begins. "What you're saying is we go back to the CDD, the place we JUST escaped from, and where all the doppelgangers are at the moment, just to find a way to get back home. WHICH, may I add, we aren't completely sure exists. Are you really willing to risk losing your wife just after you found her again?"

"We'll bring Mary with us," Simon suggests. "And we can try to close the barrier on the other, so that Geno is stuck here."

"Do you think that after this, after you kill Geno, your life will go back to normal?" Barney asks. Simon turns his head and looks at Barney's stoic expression. Simon licks his lips. "You're dead to the people in your world."

"Yes, I know," Simon says.

"I won't let you kill Geno," Barney says. "At least not now."

"I'd like to see you try, Barney," Simon says back. Barney crosses his arms and legs. "I really would."

"Fine, not like I care," Barney yells, slamming his fist on the table and standing up from his seat.

"Simon," Marcus says softly. "This plan...might not work."

"What do you know?" Simon yells. "You're basically a kid."

"He's smarter than you'll EVER be," Barney

screams at Simon. His eyes go bloodshot, and his neck pusles with red flashes. "I'm leaving."

Barney aggressively swallows the rest of his drink and storms out of the room, the wooden planks creaking under his steps. Marcus jumps up and runs after him. Barney opens the front door, walking out as Marcus grabs his shoulder and spins him around. The moonlight above glows a soft white, and illuminates the dark land around them.

"What?" Barney yells.

"I'm coming with you," Marcus says.

"No."

"Why, Barney?"

"It's dangerous," Barney responds. "I can't protect you."

"If it's dangerous, then why are you leaving?" Marcus asks. He lowers his arm down to his side. The wind blows around them, and the sound of the moving trees dances through their ears.

"Because I have to," Barncy says. He turns his back to Marcus, walking down the hill into the forest. The wind blows through Marcus' hair as he watches from the house. Barney disappears into the distant tree line, and Marcus sighs and walks back into the house. Simon picks up all the silverware and cups, lowering them into the kitchen sink in the next room.

"Get some rest, guys," he says as he turns the water on. Marcus takes a seat next to Janus, who picks at his nails. "Tomorrow we leave for the CDD."

"Are you serious, Simon?" Marcus annoyingly asks. He holds a hand over his eyes. "Barney JUST left and you're worried about going BACK to the CDD?"

Simon shuts the water off and turns around.

"No," he begins. "I'm worried about getting back home. Don't you want to go back too?"

"Of course I do," Marcus responds. He puts his arms on the table. "But we need everyone."

"If Barney isn't willing to do whatever it takes to get home, then he doesn't deserve to go home," Simon states. Marcus slams a fist down on the table.

"ARE YOU HEARING YOURSELF RIGHT NOW?" he yells. "You're just like Geno. You're too ignorant to see it."

"And how would you know that?" Simon asks. Marcus opens his mouth to speak, but closes it after a second.

"Sometimes you need to do the wrong thing to do good," Simon says. He turns back around and resumes washing dishes. Marcus holds his hands together.

"Do you think killing Geno will be a good thing?" Janus asks.

"Geno is a monster," Simon says. "He needs to be taken care of. "We need some rest. We leave for the CDD come morning."

"I'll show you all to your rooms," Mary says. She walks over to Simon, and places a hand on his back. "Let's go to sleep."

- February 7th, 1979 -

Geno stands by the same table he always does, in the same room he's always in. The screen below him shows a total scan of the world beyond the portal. A few red dots blink on the spinning globe. Each one represents a lifeform, whether it be a human or animal. One of the dots blinks in the digital model of the CDD. Geno watches it with intent.

"Sir," one of the scientists says, running into the room. Geno looks up at the black-haried girl, who hands him a manilla folder. Geno opens it up to see pages upon pages of documents about multiple things. "I collected all the letters and prints that have been received today."

"And?" Geno booms. The girl takes a deep breath.

"President Carter accepted the government funding proposition," the girl explains. "That's what the hand-written letters are. The documents are reports coming back from people that went through the portal in our tests last week. There's no signs of diseases, viruses, or death on the other side."

"So, we can fund our next few projects?" Geno asks. The girl quickly nods.

"Yes, Project Salvator-II, Worlds Collide, everything," she says. "They'll be giving us a few million per fiscal year, according to the letters."

"Good, good," Geno says. "Thank you for this information, it's very good news."

"And we have someone in the other world right now," she continues. Geno's eyebrows raise. "They're exploring the other CDD, and the atmosphere is JUST like ours. It has all of the tech and machinery we have…all for free."

"So, we have two CDD Operation Centers?" Geno asks. He flips through the papers again, finding a printed scan of the other world's status. All of the readings match the Earth, and nothing raises any alarm. "Well, what are we waiting for? We need to populate that place!"

"Also, sir," the girl cuts in. "We found a barrier…in the basement."

"A barrier?"

"It goes right into the other world," she answers. "And we've sent people through, and they've come back the same. It's in this cave underneath the lobby, about eighty yards down."

"Has anyone come out of it?" Geno asks.

"Well…one person."

"Who?"

"A doctor," the girl responds. "He may…have known your father."

Geno gasps and takes a step back, looking at the screen to see the blinking dot in the CDD gone. He looks up to the girl as his eyes widen and his mouth gapes open. He shakes his hand up, pointing at her.

"Bring him…to me. I need to know who he is. Bring him now. Now. NOW!"

18

Father's Day

"This is the CDD," Geno says.

By his side is Janus Wrench, beaten and bruised by Geno on their way here. Geno wipes some blood from his black suit, staining his already-blood covered knuckles. A door in front of them slides upward into the ceiling, and Janus' head flashes with memories. He can't tell if they are his or someone else's. He grabs onto his head and wiggles around the dirty white tile floor. His torn skin ripples with pain.

"Get a hold of yourself," Geno screams out. He grabs onto Janus' hair and pulls him up. Janus screams from the pulling and pain from the memories. He stumbles to his feet and his vision goes in and out of blur. "Walk forward."

"Why…did you bring me…here," Janus cries out as the memories fade for a bit. Geno pushes him forward into the hallway beyond the door, and the buzzing lights stab into his eyes. His broken feet bleed as he walks on his wounds.

"This is where your father is," Geno explains. He

grabs onto Janus' ear and pulls him down the left path.

"Fa…ther," Janus cries out. In his brain he sees an image of Simon Wrench and his mother, Mary Wrench. They fade as pulses of pain shoot through his head. "Save me…."

"Come on, boy," Geno yells out. Janus' eyes close as he pushes the pain into the back of his head and tries to invision his parents again. Their silhouette begins to appear like a ghost fading into view. However, Geno throws Janus to the ground in front of him and the vision fizzles away.

"Wait here, boy, and I'll get your father," Geno says. Janus looks around at the claustrophobic cream-colored padded cell he lies in. Geno exits the room, slamming a padded door behind him. Janus lays on the floor in a fetal position, trying to see his parents again. He tries to force the image, and his veins bulge out of his forehead.

Geno walks around to a metal door, which leads into a small room, where a singular scientist sits on a rolling chair. A large one-way window peers into the cell, where Geno watches Janus almost shit himself trying to see in his mind.

"Dr. Peterson," Geno says. The scientist rolls around, flipping a few switches around the room. The man looks exactly like Simon Wrench, with fluffy black hair, a large complexion, thick framed glasses, and a neckbeard.

"Yes, sir?" he responds, continuing to fly around.

119

"The boy out there is going to think you are his father," Geno explains. "I want you to be as horrible to him as possible."

Dr. Peterson stops moving. His arm hovers around a lever. He turns around, the chair leaning forward with him.

"Why, sir? He looks beaten enough, I think-"

"How DARE you question me," Geno yells. His face turns red and veins appear in his neck. He points directly at Dr. Peterson's face. "Just. Do. It."

"Sorry sir," Dr. Peterson says. He looks down at the polished floor and stands up. His face grows worried and horrified at the command. "Right away, sir."

He walks past Geno, who walks right up to the glass, his arms behind his back. Dr. Peterson walks into the room, and the voices are slightly muffled from the glass. Dr. Peterson walks up to Janus, and helps him onto his feet. Geno's smile drops immediately.

"Father…is that you?" Janus calls out as he opens his eyes. He can feel the warmth of his father help him up.

"Yes, it-," Dr. Peterson starts as Geno slams down on a glowing red button. An alarm blasts out, which shatters Dr. Peterson's eardrums. He screams out loud as he remembers his command. He drops Janus to the ground. "Who are you?"

"Father," Janus cries from the floor. He stares out straight at the wall, which is where Geno watches out from. "I'm your son."

Dr. Peterson hesitates for a moment, but he can feel Geno's gaze upon him. He wipes some sweat from his forehead.

"Oh yes, it seems that you are my son," Dr. Peterson whimpers.

"I can't believe it...I finally found you," Janus yells out in an excited tone. "I thought you were dead! Can you please help me...my legs and vision are going very quickly."

Dr. Peterson manages to pull Janus up by his collar, and holds him up. Janus' eyes begin to fill with a smoky cloud that blocks his pupils out. Dr. Peterson feels Geno's eyes watching him as Janus holds his arms out, attempting to hug his father. Dr. Peterson pushes him away, and Janus crashes down once more. Dr. Peterson gulps and sweat moistens his hair.

"What are you doing?" Janus cries out. He holds onto one of his elbows, which begins to bleed onto the padding.

"Why...why would I want a hug from y-you," Dr. Peterson lets out.

"I'm...your son," Janus responds, his voice shaking. A tear forms in his right eye, now blind from pain. Dr. Peterson lets out a condescending cough.

"Son?" he yells out. "Look at you dressed up in some ridiculous costume. Why would I EVER want a son like you?"

Janus' mind stops. All he can see is black, in and

out of his head. What did he do? Why is his father saying all these things…what is going on?

"You are NOTHING to me."

Janus' pain fizzles, but his wounds grow.

"I don't want anything to do with you."

Janus' head looks up at the ceiling, where he can feel the warmth of the light above him. Even the image of his father isn't appearing anymore. Everything is just black…and the light above him begins to grow cold.

"You are not my son anymore."

Janus' heart stops. His body scrunches up and he screams out at the top of his lungs. A small crack forms right in front of Geno's face. It brings a smile to his face. Janus' arms contort around and veins pop all over his body.

"JUST SHUT THE FUCK UP ALREADY!" Dr. Peterson yells out, trying to outdo Janus' blood curdling scream. "YOU WILL NEVER BE MY SON! YOU ARE WORTHLESS! YOU MEAN NOTHING TO ME!"

Janus' voice cracks and shatters as blood pools in his mouth. Dr. Peterson swiftly turns around and slams the door shut behind him. He collapses to the ground and lays in a puddle of his own sweat. He breathes heavily as his heart pulls down his body. He can still hear Janus from beyond the soundproof room.

"How did it go?" Geno asks, his dress shoes clacking against the tiles. "I'll talk to him later, give him a walkie talkie, and send him on his way. You did a good job, Dr. Peterson."

"Why...did you make me do that?" Dr. Peterson cries out. His skin is deathly pale and his eyes dart around the hallway. He doesn't try to stand from the floor.

"That was the son of Simon Wrench," Geno explains. He crouches down next to Dr. Peterson. "My old partner."

"Why did you make me do that, Geno?" Dr. Peterson asks again. Geno's face turns to anger. He grabs onto Dr. Peterson's fluff of hair, pulling his head up to face him.

"What did you call me?" Geno whispers. "You don't use my name like that, you understand?"

"I'm sorry sir, I didn't mean it," Dr. Peterson says as his eyes meet with Geno's. Geno's grip on Dr. Peterson's hair grows.

"You are a doppelganger of Simon Wrench, so I decided to use that to get back at him," Geno explains. "Your son...is his son's doppel. Janus Peterson and Simon Wrench are our enemies because they KNOW about us."

"Sir, Janus Peterson is just a kid...," Dr. Peterson says with a smirk. "He can't be that bad, right?"

"Dr. Peterson, Simon Wrench is still alive."

Geno drops Dr. Peterson's face to the ground, and his nose cracks and bleeds. Geno wipes his hands together and stands up. He pulls a napkin from his suit pocket and drops it on Dr. Peterson's head.

"You'll be needing this. And get back to work."

Geno steps over Dr. Peterson and walks into the room where Janus Wrench is. Dr. Peterson hears the screaming start again as the door comes to a slamming close.

19

Fate Comes

arney walks through the forest, following random dirt paths of unknown origin. He kicks rocks around, annoyed at everything for no reason. The air is still and so are the trees around him, which gives him a sense of wrong. His mind runs with the guilt of leaving, but he knows it is for the best.

"Stupid Simon…," he says to himself. He kicks a large rock past a tree, and it splashes into a small pond. "What the hell does he think he's doing?"

"Barney…," a voice calls out. Barney quickly turns around and scans the area. He looks back toward the way he came, where he sees himself copying the same movements he's doing. It's a doppelganger of Barney, wearing the same homeless outfit, with the same greasy hair, and the same unwashed face.

"You better stay back, doppelganger!" Barney yells out.

"You think I'm one? You look like one of those elongated ones," the other Barney yells back. He pulls out a shiv from his torn jacket. The blade shines in the gloomy light. Normal Barney stares his doppelganger down, as the doppelganger's head is popped like a balloon. Blood splatters everywhere, and the body falls to the ground. The knife dives down and slices into the dirt, where it stands straight up.

"Ron, Ron, Ron," Martin Geno says, walking out from behind a tree. A handful of guards follow behind. He walks out clapping, laughing to himself, as he steps over the doppelganger's body. "We've missed you."

—

Marcus jumps out of his bed, sweating profusely and gasping for air. The room is dark, and a light glow comes from the closed window to his right. He grasps his chest, and closes his eyes. After a few seconds of catching his breath, he sighs.

"I need to go get Barney," he says to himself. He slides out of bed, putting on his sneakers and tiptoeing through the room. Passing through the room, he walks into the hallway and looks down both sides. The cabin wood walls hum with soft wind songs, and the moonlight outside shines upon the dark trees. He carefully walks to the front door, making sure not to creak any floorboards. He touches the doorknob and as he turns it, someone coughs behind him. He jumps, and turns to see Janus holding a yellow candle.

"Where are you going?" Janus asks.

"I'm going to find Barney," Marcus explains.

"We're going to find him in the morning," Janus

says. "It's the middle of the night."

Marcus sighs.

"That's too long, Janus. He could die out there."

"So what?" Janus yells. "Who cares?"

"Do you hear yourself?" Marcus says, moving away from the door and toward Janus. "What are you saying? Barney is our friend."

"You mean YOUR friend," Janus says, holding up a finger toward him. His face drops and his eyebrows bend down. "You've been clinging to him this whole time. Barely talked to me at all. And besides, we have Simon who is much stronger and smarter."

"Are you getting jealous right now?" Marcus asks, his skin growing red. He walks right up to Janus, and towers over him.

"Yes, I am!" Janus yells at him, shoving the candle in his face. "You're my only friend! And Barney is going to steal you from me!"

"What are you TALKING ABOUT?" Marcus yells, his voice growing louder. "You're making it sound like we're dating!"

"No, I didn't mean it like that!" Janus quickly spits out. "We've been friends forever, and now Barney is here, you've only been talking to him. You're all I have left, Marcus."

"If you're too scared to find Barney," Marcus says, his voice going back to normal. "Why don't you just go home with Simon."

Janus stands quiet for a moment. The hot wax from the candle drips over his fingers, but he doesn't feel it. Janus looks down, and Marcus turns away.

"You know what…," Janus finally says. Marcus walks back to the door. He turns the knob and opens it, letting the wind fill the room. Janus' hair flows around. "Go get yourself killed and see if I care."

Janus turns and walks away, placing the candle down on the metal plate he got it from. Marcus hesitates for a moment before walking out into the forest outside. The sounds of crickets fill Marcus' ears, and the smell of grass and river water fill his nose. He walks into the forest as a shadowy figure passes by. The thing jumps from tree to tree, sneaking up on the cabin house.

Simon opens his eyes and yawns, waking up Mary. He stretches out of bed and scratches his ass as he walks over to the bedroom bathroom. He opens the wooden door and walks into the dark room. He reaches around the wall for the light switch, and when he flicks it on he sees the shower curtain move. He slowly walks over to the solid white curtains, putting his hand out and moving it to the side. Behind it, a figure crouches down on the shower floor, holding a knife in his hand.

"Barney?" Simon asks. The figure breathes heavily, and is cast in shadow. Its eyes look like little white dots. Simon fully pushes the curtain to the side, and a golden mask is revealed. "Who the fuck are you?"

"Father…," the man says. "It is me…your son."

"Janus?" Simon cries out. He kneels next to the shower, looking at the golden mask on his son's face. Janus Wrench wears all black beside the mask. He dangles the knife in his hands, staring at it with his white pupils. "What happened to you? When did they take you?"

"I am seeing double," Janus says through the mask. "I see everything. I have all the eyes in the world."

"What is going on?" Simon asks. His voice is worried and scared, and he tries to lean closer to his son. Janus Wrench's pupils look up at Simon, and his fingers clench onto the knife.

"You are not my father anymore," Janus says.

"What?" Simon says as Janus lunges forward, cutting Simon's left eye with the knife. He screams and falls backward, clutching his eye with both hands. He yells out in pain and kicks around, trying to hit Janus. "YOU ARE NOT MY SON!"

"The truth keeps coming out...," Janus Wrench says, standing over Simon's struggling body. He holds the knife with both hands and holds it up above his head. "Happy Father's Day, dad."

He thrusts it down, and a leg kicks his hands right before the knife stabs Simon. The knife flies into the wall, slamming into the mirror on the wall. Janus Wrench jumps up to see Janus Peterson standing in the doorway, with Mary right behind. Janus' forehead bursts with veins and the skin is completely red, but Janus lives through the pain.

"Ssssssssooooo," Janus Wrench says, hissing like a

snake. "You think you can jusssst....replace me like a doppelganger! I guess my father really DID move on."

Janus Peterson steps over Simon, picking up the knife on the ground and pointing it toward Janus Wrench. Mary quickly bends down and pulls Simon out of the bathroom, closing the door behind them. Janus Wrench zips down his black bodysuit, pulling out another knife from an inside pocket. This one seems more like a sharpened slab of jagged metal than an actual knife.

"You keep coming back for me," Janus Peterson says, walking around the room in a circle. Janus Wrench walks opposite of him.

"You keep getting in my way," Janus Wrench responds. He leans over as he walks. Janus Peterson smirks, and steps onto the white porcelain toilet.

"You wanna brawl? Let's brawl," Janus Peterson says as he lunges forward off the toilet into Janus Wrench, crashing into the tiled wall. They both fall down onto the carpet, cushioning their fall. Janus Peterson shoves the knife into Janus Wrench's gut, but he is unmoved. Janus Wrench grabs onto Janus Peterson's head, holding it up above the shower wall and slamming it down a few times. Peterson groans every time he hits the wall.

"You replace me, I replace YOU!" Janus Wrench yells. Peterson grabs onto Wrench's hand, twisting it backward and cracking the bone. Wrench's mask is covered in splattering blood as Peterson cracks his arm back. "What are you doing?"

"Recycling you!" Peterson yells out. He grabs onto Wrench's face, slamming it into the wall until the tiles are folded inward. Blood pools onto the ground as shards of tile are lodged deeper into Wrench's brain. One of his white pupils dims into black. Peterson tosses Wrench's body into the glass sink, which breaks, as he stands up and brushes off the dust and dirt.

Outside, Mary tears some material off a blanket, tying it around Simon's head. The blue cloth stains immediately, but is able to stop the blood flow. Mary lays Simon down on the bed, letting him rest for a moment. They can hear the chaos going on in the bathroom from outside the door.

"Simon?" she softly asks. "What is going on?"

"We need to go, Mary," Simon responds. He keeps both eyes closed. "It's not safe."

"Why is our son attacking you?"

"It's not…it's a doppelganger," Simon answers. "I don't even know if Janus is still alive."

"What about the new boy? Janus Peterson?" Mary asks. Simon laughs.

"He's too skinny to be a Wrench," Simon jokes. "I'm sure Geno got to him right after we disappeared."

"What happened to everything, Simon?" Mary asks. "Why must our lives be ruined?"

"I don't know, Mary," Simon whispers. "I don't know."

Janus Peterson opens the door, and lets it slam into

the wall. He's covered in blood and dust, and his hair is stuck to the back of his neck. He steps out, and drops the knife from his hand. He falls to his knees, and lets out a long sigh.

"Whenever I see him…my head races," Janus says. He looks up at the ceiling, raising his arms up. "WHY!"

He looks at Simon, who is laying on the bed heavily wounded. Janus pushes on his knees, quickly standing up and running to Simon's side. He looks at Simon's face, which is covered in dried blood and the makeshift eyepatch.

"Is he ok?" Janus quickly asks.

"He's fine," Mary answers. "Luckily, the cut wasn't too deep so he doesn't need stitches, or anything. I'm more worried about the man in the bathroom."

"He said something about me being a doppelganger…," Janus explains. "He's gone now, so he won't be much of a problem."

"We need to get going," Simon says through the conversation. Mary sits on the bed next to him, putting her hand on his forehead.

"You need to get better," Mary says. "And you need rest."

"We need to escape this world," Simon says.

"He's right," Janus agrees.

"Go get Marcus, and we can leave for the CDD one last time."

"Oh," Janus says. "About that."

Simon turns his head toward Janus, who rubs the back of his neck.

"Where is Marcus?" Simon asks.

"About Marcus…," Janus says, stretching his words out. "He sort of…left."

"What do you mean 'he left?'" Mary asks. Simon shakes his head.

"He went to go find Barney," Janus says. He quickly throws out the words and Simon yells.

"You know what!" he cries out to the ceiling. "I don't care anymore! If they both want to leave alone and kill themselves, then they can go ahead and do that."

Simon looks over at Janus.

"We're leaving tomorrow. With or without them."

20

An Alliance

Marcus crouches down, sneaking by the CDD's gray halls. The vent cover from earlier was still open, so he decided to let himself in.

Once he reached the broken couch room, he exited through the door on his right. He watches his back, making sure nobody comes up behind him. He knows of the danger he is in currently, but he knows it's for the best.

"Where do I even look?" Marcus whispers to himself. "He could be anywhere."

Marcus approaches a corner, where he hears two voices on the other side. He shimmies along the wall, pushing his back against it. A drip of sweat runs down his back, and he watches as some shadows dance along the wall next to him. He listens in to the conversation as he holds his breath.

"I'm glad you came back," Geno's voice says to a mysterious figure. "I heard you want to make a deal?"

"My mother is still alive…and out there somewhere," the figure says. Marcus realizes it's that crazy bitch trying to kill them. "And I keep seeing the same people over and over again."

"Do you want to kill them?" Geno asks.

"Yes," the doppelganger responds. "They keep trying to hurt me."

"Am I speaking to Janus Wrench right now?" Geno asks. Marcus thinks to himself about the name.

"Yes," the doppelganger answers. "They want to hurt me. I don't want to die."

Marcus leans his head ever so slightly forward, turning it so he can see Geno and the doppelganger, who dons a sculpted golden mask and a yellow hazmat suit. Dried blood stains the material. Geno reaches into his inside suit pocket, pulling out a sharp object and handing it to the doppelganger.

"If you take this, and kill your father and the bad people," Geno says. "Then you can be free in the happy world."

"Thank you," the doppelganger says. He bows before Geno, and holds the elongated kitchen knife in his hand. "And you must kill Uncle Ron as well, but not before the worlds collide."

"Yes, Geno," the doppelganger responds. Marcus quickly turns back behind the wall, breathing heavily and looking down his right to make sure no guard has found him yet.

"They're gonna kill Simon and Janus...," he says to himself. "I need to get out of here and warn them. What if they left already? Shit!"

"Did you hear that?" Geno asks. The question

135

sends shivers down Marcus' spine, and goosebumps grow across his body. Geno's shoes tap the tiles below, and his shadow grows on the wall. Marcus can feel Geno right at the edge of the corner when the footsteps stop. Marcus waits for a moment, holding his breath until his skin turns purple.

"Must have been nothing," Geno says. He turns around and begins walking away, and Marcus waits another second before opening his mouth and gasping for air. A hand violently grabs his forehead from the other side of the corner, and it smashes his head against the wall. Marcus falls to the ground in pain as the back of his head bleeds out. His vision blurs and he turns onto his back, seeing the doppelganger walk over to him.

He stands over Marcus, dangling the knife by two fingers. Marcus reaches his hand up, and Geno steps into view and slaps it away. He slams one of his fancy, shining shoes onto Marcus' chest, pushing down on his ribs. Geno leans over and stares down at Marcus.

"Who may you be?" Geno laughs. "You're one of the ones that keep coming back, escaping, coming back, etcetera."

"Fuck you," Marcus says, struggling to lift up a middle finger as his left eye closes. Geno slaps the hand away again, and it slams onto the ground. "Where is Barney?"

"Don't play games with me, boy," Geno yells out at Marcus. Geno points a finger into his face. "I am Martin

Geno, and you are working with Simon Wrench. He's a liar, cheater, and a fiend. You can join me, and save yourself."

"Fuck-," Marcus starts, and Geno shoves an entire hand into Marcus' mouth. Marcus chokes on the fingers, blood and spit both flying from his mouth. He mumbles something, but can't let out any words. Geno sighs and shoves his hand down more, which causes Marcus to violently vomit all over Geno. He shakes his head and grabs onto Marcus' tongue. He pushes his trimmed nails into the flesh, and cuts along the back.

"You won't be needing this," Geno states as he pulls a thin layer of flesh off of Marcus' tongue, as he tries to slap Geno away. Marcus throws his hands up, failing to hit Geno in the face. "It may help you to shut your fucking mouth once in a while, you fat fucking moron."

He pulls the flesh off like a blanket off a mouse, and shakes his puke and blood covered hand to get some of it off. He holds up the flesh, as if it's a little flesh condom. He hands it to the doppelganger, who puts it in his hazmat suit. Marcus sits on his back, mouth full of barf and blood. He chokes on it and he begins to convulse. Geno rolls his eyes and kicks Marcus onto his side, and all the mixture in his mouth pools out onto the floor as he coughs and gasps for air. His mouth burns from his tongue, and it feels as though he has tacks all around his mouth and no matter what, they're poking into him.

"Geno?" Marcus can hear Barney ask from down

the hall. As he tries to keep his right eye open, he loses consciousness and passes out. Geno clicks his fingers and the doppelganger picks up Marcus, turns the corner and walks out of view. Barney runs up to Geno, and as he stops he leans over and catches his breath.

"Yes, Ron?" Geno asks as he looks down on Barney. "What do you want?"

"Sorry, I just ran all the way from the finance room," Barney says between heavy breaths. "The government is sending us less and less with every check."

"WHAT?" Geno yells out, echoing down the hallway. His face instantly rushes red, and his eyes almost bulge right out of their sockets. He rushes past Barney, who jogs backward to keep up. "Why? Did they say WHY?"

"Yes, sir," Barney responds. "And that's the problem. They want the public to know who's running the place now. It's a new law that was put in place."

"Fuck," Geno cries out in anger. They traverse the halls toward the front lobby, where laughter and chatter fills the room. "EVERYONE! GET YOUR ASSES TO WORK!"

All the scientists and guards rush around, with Geno walking straight through them toward the golden elevator. He stops right before the doors open, turning to Barney and grabbing him by his collar.

"Get back to your assignment, and I'll be back when I can," Geno says. Barney nods and runs off as Geno lets go. The elevator doors swing open, and Geno steps into the shaky room. He turns and presses on the down button, which is right under the up button. The down arrow glows as the doors swing closed, and bring Geno down to the barrier room.

—

"Mr. President," Martin Geno says softly, walking into the oval office. The round room is illuminated by the calm moonlight outside, and a few candles here and there. He walks over the blue carpet and the presidential seal, taking a calm seat on one of the cream colored chairs. He crosses his legs, admiring the white floral wallpaper, antique wood decorations, and the portraits of famous presidents from past decades. Behind the polished brown presidential desk, an American flag hangs next to the yellow curtains.

"Mr. Geno," Bill Clinton says as he turns around in his chair. He organizes a few papers on his desk, placing them next to a navy blue pen. His fair blue eyes pop along with his glistening silver hair. He dons a seamless black suit, along with a white button-down undershirt and a polka-dotted monochrome tie. "I see you have come to ask about the government funding, yes?"

"Yes," Geno nods. Bill opens one of the drawers on his desk, pulling out a letter and placing it on his desk.

"So, tell me," Bill starts. "What are you concerned with?"

"As you know, I run the Center of Developmental

Design, after the disappearance of Simon Wrench," Geno explains. He places his hands on his crossed legs. "I've said that I am still working there as a higher up, but I cannot say that I own the company."

"Why not?" Bill asks. He places his hands on the desk and leans forward. "You made the company with him, why not take action and rise above?"

"Mr. President, respectfully, don't you think it's rude to take over someone's role?" Geno asks. He's completely lying, he doesn't want to come forward until he knows Simon is dead and cannot spill the truth. "Simon could still be out there. People will riot if they hear me tell everyone that I am washing Simon's achievements away."

"Mr. Geno, you are thinking too much into this. The people need to know who we are giving money to, not what," Bill explains. "It's the people that matter, not necessarily the institutions. We could fund a science lab, but if the people found out a rapist or a murderer ran it, there would be riots. You need to rise above and take credit. You are a good man."

"Yes, Mr. President," Geno says through a forced smile. He bows his head and stands up, wiping his suit jacket. Bill gives him a reaffirming smile as Geno walks across the room toward the door. Geno turns his head away, and rubs his sweaty forehead. He opens the door, and walks out.

21

Betrayal

"How'd you sleep?"

Janus Peterson awakens on a soft mattress. His arms lay down by his side, and he sees Simon Wrench sitting on a woven basket in the corner. The baby blue wallpaper peels around the shining window. Janus yawns as he tosses the fluffy white blanket to his feet. His hair feels greasy, and his clothes feel lived-in, but he's content.

"Have you been here all night?" Janus asks. Simon lets out a hearty laugh and pushes on his legs to stand up. He towers over the bookcases and furniture dotted around the room. He walks over to the door, where Janus sees Mary rush past.

"Are you ready to go?" Simon asks.

"Yeah, I guess," Janus responds. He slowly hops out of the bed as he wipes the sleep from his eyes. Simon notices Janus is visibly upset, as he walks out of the room with his head down. Simon grabs his shoulder and stops him.

"What's wrong, Janus?" Simon comfortably asks. "We're going home, you should be excited."

Janus shrugs, shaking his head. Simon lets go of his shoulder and leans against the doorframe.

"Going home without Marcus…it just doesn't feel right," Janus explains. "I know it was his decision to go out and find Barney, but we can't give up on him. At least I can't."

"I know, Janus, but we need to save ourselves first, and then we can come back and get Marcus and Barney," Simon tries to say. "We're in serious trouble right now, and we need to do whatever we can to get OUT of it."

"I still don't think it's right. If we see any sign of either of them," Janus says. "We are going to change our goal."

"Sounds good," Simon says. They both walk out to join Mary on the porch. Outside, a storm rages on with heavy winds dragging trees down and a flurry of rain shooting through leaves. The three prepare to walk as Geno's internal rage stops for a moment.

"Your name is Marcus, right?" Geno asks in a pitch-black room. Marcus opens his eyes to see nothing, but his panicking voice and struggles to break free are clearly heard. Marcus feels some sort of wet rag shoved into his mouth, and it tastes of grime and sweat. "I knew a Marcus once…he's gone now."

Geno clicks on the lights, which illuminate the yellow-stained padded walls, and Marcus' eyes adjust to the light. He spastically throws his head around, looking at the greasy room, and at the metal chair he's tied with rope to. Geno walks over to Marcus from the dark corner of the room, removing the rag with two fingers.

"What do you want?" Marcus yells out as Geno removes the towel. Spit flies onto Geno's sleeve. He wipes it off.

"I found your little safehouse, and I noticed that nobody was there," Geno laughs. It's clear he's laughing to taunt Marcus. "I know you came with people. And I need one of them. I can leave you and your partners alive, or at least alive for the most part, but I am to believe you have Simon Wrench with you."

"Fuck. You," Marcus yells as he spits again at Geno, this time aiming at his face. Geno takes a deep breath as he wipes his face, and then he raises his right hand up. "Give me your best shot, motherfucker."

Geno lowers his hand at incredible speed, hitting Marcus so hard that he and the chair fly into the wall, bouncing off the padding. A few flakes of yellow grime fall to the floor. Geno walks over and picks Marcus up by his hair.

"YOU STUPID FUCKING PIG!" he yells right into Marcus' face. "Don't you DARE spit at me EVERY AGAIN!"

He slams Marcus' face down.

"Or I swear to God, I'll have your head on my fucking wall. Now tell me, where is Simon Wrench?"

The door creaks open, and Barney runs into the room. He tries to speak to Geno, but stops when he sees

Marcus on the ground, spitting out blood. He crouches down, and attempts to lift Marcus and his chair up, but Geno slaps Barney's neck.

"Ron, what do you think you're doing?" Geno exclaims. His skin boils red and spit covers his mouth. Barney lets go of Marcus, who falls again, and stands up with his hands up. "You pathetic pig, leave him so we can use him for experimenting. If he won't tell us where Simon is, then we can at least use his dead body."

"Yes sir, I'll go ahead and prep his room," Barney says, bowing before Geno and running over to the door. Marcus coughs out some blood, and Barney pauses as he touches the door's metal handle.

"Barney," Marcus says, his voice slurred. Barney turns his head to see Marcus flipping him off from his tied arms. "So you're not Barney? You're Ron?"

"I can expla-," Barney starts.

"No, no, no," Marcus cuts him off. "Don't bother. I've already accepted you as a lie."

"Marcus, I-"

"Just stop talking," Marcus yells. "It makes sense why you didn't want Simon killing Geno. I thought you were a good person with questionable morals...but no. You just didn't want it to happen because you are Geno's lap dog. You bow to him. You're a fucking slave."

"Marcus," Ron says. "I wanted to tell you. I wanted to tell you all. I'm bound by contract, where I must serve him no matter what. If I break it, my family will be killed."

Geno smiles as he knows it's true.

"I trusted you," Marcus cries out. "And you went and threw it all away. I don't even believe your little sob story, you piece of shit. Leave me to die here. I don't want your face to be the last I see."

"I'm sorry, Marcus," Ron says. He walks over to Marcus and pats him on his shoulder. Marcus feels something slide out of Ron's sleeve and he can sense it crawl down his back. Ron turns around and walks out of the room, closing the door behind him. Marcus feels around for the item, which cuts one of his fingers when he grabs it.

"Now, you sit here and wait for us to finish prepping your room," Geno says, his crooked smile annoying Marcus. "I'm sure Simon will come save you, but I hope that happens."

With one final fake laugh, Geno walks out the door, and Marcus waits until the sound of footsteps fades away. He moves himself onto his stomach, the weight of the chair pushing down on him. He feels the knife fall to the ground, and he pushes his arms further into the binds to grab it. Once he has it in hand, he turns it around and awkwardly slices through the rope, which takes him a few minutes.

He frees one arm, and is easily able to cut open the other. He wipes his nose and covers it from the musty smell of the room. He runs toward the door and slowly opens it, peeking out in order to check for anyone outside.

The coast is clear, so he steps out and hugs the wall. He takes the knife out of his pocket, checking out the sharpened bark that was stabbed into Simon earlier.

"Why would he give me this?" Marcus asks himself. He looks down the brown hallway, thinking to himself about what to do next. "I have to save Ron from Geno."

22

The Portal Room

The trio climbs from the golf cart. They stand before the massive building that is the CDD, one that Simon has gone in and out of too many times. Simon, Mary, and Janus all stand next to each other. A portrait of a broken family, one broken by Geno. To Simon, Geno broke the family but will one day bring it back together somehow. They stare at the gray visage, where the yellow letter of 'CDD' shines in the sun. The clouds have gone away, and now the blue sky shows its face.

"This is it," Simon says, breaking the silence. "We're going home."

"Do we even know where the portal is?" Janus asks. Simon turns his head toward him. "I mean, we've been around the whole base pretty much."

"Well," Simon responds. "We just have to find the portal room. There has to be a way to find out where it is. Let's go."

The trio takes the same path they did the first time they went to the CDD; through the vent, past the reception desk, and out into the brown wood halls. The lights flicker with a yellow glow, and the walls are smeared with blood. Corpses line the ground, covered in flies and emitting a smell of rot and shit. They walk down the left side of the hall, where they enter the golden lobby. Janus walks up to the map, where he studies all of the rooms and paths.

"Do you think they'll just label it 'Portal Room,' or something?" Janus asks.

"Janus, don't be stupid. Of course they wouldn't do that," Simon responds. He looks at the map, and it shows an elevator leading down to nothing. That elevator is in that very room.

"I was just messing around, you don't have to call me stupid," Janus says as he puts his hands on his waist.

"You're right, I'm sorry," Simon says. "Where do you think this elevator leads to?"

Janus turns around, seeing the golden wall with a slit down the middle. He looks over to Simon and Mary, before realizing Mary is gone.

"Where's Mary?" Janus asks. Simon turns to his wife, who he realizes is gone as well.

"She was…just right here," he responds. "Maybe she walked away?"

"Let's just go on this elevator and see where it takes us," Janus says. They both board the shining chamber, which takes them down. The ride is smooth and they don't even realize the elevator is actually moving. The door opens, and leads into a short, dimly lit hall with one door at the end and one on either side of the walls. The walls are gray and covered in black streaks, and a smell of burning rises from beneath the grate floors.

"Where are we?" Simon asks. He walks over to the metal left door, pushing it open into a blinding white room with a singular wooden table in the middle. Simon walks over, brushing his hand across the dust covered sand-colored wood. He slowly paces around it, looking down at the papers covering the desk. He leans over, picking up a document that is stained with coffee rings and drool. The note reads:

M. Geno,

Project [WORLDS COLLIDE] is almost complete. We've created a device that will pull both universes, {EARTH-A & EARTH-B}, together, causing the space matter to combine into one. If successful, [EARTH-A] will have the same conditions as [EARTH-B], excluding the [S-12 VIRUS]. If this fails, it could cause both universes to collide into each other on a jagged line, destroying everything in both Earths. Please know there is a low chance of this happening, but a chance nonetheless.

Dr. Peterson

"Glad you could make it," Geno's voice says from behind Simon. He turns around to see Geno closing the door behind him, dressed in his fanciest red suit with a white tie. He holds his fingers together and crosses his legs.

"Martin," Simon says through gritted teeth.

"Simon."

"What is this all about?"

"A little…experiment I've been conducting," Geno says, stepping forward toward Simon. Simon crumbles the paper in his hands, throwing it onto the ground and crushing it beneath his foot.

"Experiment?" Simon screams at Geno. "This could kill EVERYONE! This isn't just an experiment."

"You're right, Simon," Geno says with a smile. Simon can't tell if it's real or fake. "It's my best experiment yet. After you and Mary disappeared, I took your son into my care. And after that, I found what seemed to be a doppelganger of young Janus. So, with the help of some scientists, we combined their structures together. So, I thought, why not do it with the world."

"You are crazy, Martin," Simon yells. "You always have been, but this? This is insane. What happened to you?"

"Shut up!" Geno screams out at Simon. He points a finger at Simon's face. "Don't you DARE talk about me like that. I've done more than you could EVER dream about."

"Well MAYBE if you would discuss it with me, maybe I could fathom your fucked up mind. I've seen things in here," Simon says. "Things I can't even think about why you would have them."

"No, you don't understand Simon," Geno says, pacing around the room. "I see things. Things...nobody will be able to understand. We're getting side tracked...Simon, my old friend. Could you ever forgive me? I guess I see the error of my ways."

Simon looks at Geno with a confused expression. His fists tighten.

"No," Simon coldly states. "What you're doing...what you're GOING to do, it's inhumane. Only something a monster would do."

Geno's face grows cold and his lips fall. He stares at Simon with a stern, killer expression. Geno's eyes are devoid of all emotion beside 'death.'

"Fine," Geno says, his voice stoic and mono. "You don't need to forgive me, but I do want to at least make up for my biggest mistake. Follow me, and I'll let you go through the portal. Back to your home, back to your life."

"I can't just leave this place knowing what you're gonna do!" Simon cries out. Geno smirks with a little chuckle.

"Then...," Geno says with a loud sigh. "You won't be able to see your real son."

Simon's eyes widen and he takes a step backward in disbelief. His heart beats and a drop of sweat drips down his face.

"R-real son?" Simon asks. He clutches his chest with his hand. Geno takes the opportunity to hurt his old partner where it hurts the most. All while smiling.

"That kid you are with…he is a doppelganger of your son," Geno says. He walks over to Simon, placing a hand on his shoulder and leaning toward him. "If you follow me, I can take you to him."

"H-how can I…," Simon tries to speak. "I trust that…you aren't l-lying about this?"

Simon's vision blurs as the sweat picks up. Geno removes the handkerchief from his suit pocket and wipes Simon's forehead with it. Simon's hand moves around the table behind him, feeling a sharp object that Geno doesn't notice.

"When have I EVER lied to you?" Geno lies to Simon. "I've been NOTHING but honest with you for years! Even about all the bad stuff."

"I don't believe you," Simon says, clutching the letter opener behind him. "After everything you've done after what I've read…how could I?"

"Come ON, Simon!" Geno yells out in annoyance, dropping his hands down to his side. "I don't hate you! I was just a little mad and made you go into that portal. Can't you just-"

Simon raises the letter opener into Geno's cheek, and pushes it right through the skin. Geno shakes and screams from the pain as Simon wiggles the knife around his wound. Geno slaps Simon across the face, who falls to the ground with a thud.

"A LITTLE MAD?" Simon yells at the top of his

lungs from the ground. "YEAH! You're RIGHT! You ARE a little mad! You made me go through that portal on PURPOSE! That was no ACCIDENT, GENO! You ruined my life just because YOU COULDN'T GET WHAT YOU WANTED!"

"Simon!" Geno yells back, pulling the bloody knife from his cheek. He spits out some skin flaps, and drops the letter opener to the ground. "You don't understand, I had no choice. You always stopped me from researching."

"Because everything you wanted to do was HORRIBLE!" Simon cries out. Geno shakes his head and turns away.

"No," Geno says to the wall. "It's necessary."

"Necessary for WHAT?" Simon asks. "What are you even trying to DO?"

"I need to know everything," Geno answers. "I need to know what my creation was thinking…what he was talking about."

"YOUR creation?" Simon asks. "Don't you mean MINE? I created The Salvator, and YOU set him free. He could be killing people again, and it's blood on YOUR hands."

"You think he's a failure, huh?" Geno responds, turning back to Simon. "No, Simon. That was our greatest achievement."

"We lost control of him," Simon says, spitting in Geno's face. The door opens, and a mutated Dr. Mengele walks in. His height has increased to about seven feet tall,

153

and he hunches over with a red band on his left arm. His clothes are tattered and covered in trash bag scraps. He walks over to Simon, grabbing him by his arms and lifting him up. "And it's your fault."

"No, Simon," Geno says, walking up to Simon. "He has your DNA in him. And soon, your son will be part Simon Wrench as well. What do you think we did to you in that surgery room? You didn't need healing. But your son does."

23

The Beginning of the End

J anus walks through the right door, opposite of the one Simon entered through. He pushes through the stiff door, walking into a bomb shelter-esque padded room, with silver empty weapon racks lining the walls. He steps across the pavement floor, past the blue tarps hanging down from the grated ceiling. In the middle of the room, an ominous light shines down on a mysterious figure sitting on a chair, covered in a sheet of clear plastic. He reaches a steady hand out, pulling the sheet down to reveal Marcus snoozing on a wooden chair. His face is covered in bumps and bruises, and one of his eyes is swollen.

"Marcus?" Janus asks. Marcus remains asleep. Janus thinks to himself for a moment before punching Marcus across the face. That wakes him up, screaming as he falls to the ground. He rubs his face as Janus looks around and whistles to avoid suspicion.

"What the hell was that for?" Marcus asks.

"Me?" Janus lies. "Why would I do such a thing?"

Marcus stares at Janus with a murderous intent as he holds his bruised cheek.

"Ok, I'm sorry," Janus says. "I needed to wake you up, man."

"What are you doing here?" Marcus asks, pushing himself up. "And why just you?"

"I'm going home, Marcus," Janus says. "I'm gonna ask the same, why are YOU here?'

"I was kidnapped by Geno," Marcus explains. He pulls the fallen chair back up and takes a seat. "And then I–wait a minute."

"Hm?" Janus murmurs.

"You were gonna leave without me?" Marcus asks with a suspicious tone. He shakes his head. "Whatever. That's not important to me right now."

"Where's Barney?" Janus asks. Marcus laughs in his face.

"You wanna know where Barney is?" Marcus says in a high voice. "His name is actually RON! And he's working for Geno, but I feel like he's not as evil as you'd think."

"What?" Janus cries in shock. He walks backward, bumping into a metal workbench.

"He needs our help, I think," Marcus says. "But, there's no time to explain. We need to find him and get out of here."

Janus nods, and they both walk out into the hallway. They peek their heads out, looking down both ways. There's nothing down toward the elevator, but when Janus looks to his right, he sees Simon entering through the far door.

"SIM-!" Janus yells, but Marcus quickly covers his mouth with his hand. The rest of Simon's name is mumbled through fingers.

"What the HELL are you doing?" Marcus yells in whispers. Simon turns his head back, looking around the hallway as Geno comes into view beyond the door. "If Geno sees us, there's no telling what he'll do to us."

"Heard something, Simon?" Geno asks.

"Thought I did," Simon responds. He closes the door as he walks through, and the two boys take a sigh of relief. They walk out into the hallway, where the sound of the elevator makes them both jump. A light above the doors signals the platform is rising to the top lobby.

"Sorry," Janus says to Marcus. "I didn't see him."

"It's fine," Marcus says back. "Luckily, he didn't hear you, but what the hell is Simon doing? Is he in on it too?"

"Maybe Geno captured him?" Janus suggests. Marcus shrugs. "But we need to go save him."

"It didn't seem like he was captured," Marcus says.

"Do you think he's still friends with Geno?" Janus asks.

"I don't know, but we're about to find out."

The last door in the hall, opposite the elevator, rests below a singular white lightbulb. The door has no window, and is a solid brick of metal. A sign on the top reads 'PORTAL ROOM,' to which Janus laughs at.

157

"Really?" he whispers. "Portal room? I can't believe that's actually the name. I thought they'd make it less obvious. He walks up to the door, pressing his ear against it.

"Do you think Geno made a deal with Simon to bring him in there?" Marcus asks. He scratches at his left sleeve.

"No," Janus says. "I don't think Simon would be that dumb. He'd never leave here without us."

"Well, should we go in?" Marcus asks. Before he finishes, a deep scream comes from the other side of the door. Janus jumps and rushes into the brick of metal, possibly shattering some bone. The door creaks open just a tiny bit, and Janus squeezes through. Marcus runs over and puts both hands on the door, pushing it open into a large underground chamber, made of natural rock formations and manmade clearings. In the middle of the room, a large glass pane glitches and pulses around, spraying blue streaks around. Geno stands before it, watching as Janus Wrench stands over Simon's fallen body. The room fills with a violent wind, which gushes around Marcus' hair.

"SIMON!" Janus yells as he runs past a large metal machine labeled 'PORTAL MACHINE.' He kicks Janus Wrench in the stomach, but Wrench catches his leg and twists him around. Janus Peterson falls to the floor, and Wrench slides him away.

Marcus runs over to Janus Wrench, punching him in his golden mask, which shatters the area around the mouth. Wrench's white pupils shudder behind the eyeholes, and Marcus puts both fists up.

"You wanna brawl, motherfucker?" he yells. He throws another punch, which Wrench catches, much to Marcus' shock. "I got more than that!"

Janus gets back up, running over to Simon and grabbing onto his arms. He pulls Simon away, and Wrench notices. Wrench throws his head forward, knocking into Marcus' nose and causing him to stumble backward.

"SIMON!" Wrench snickers. "HE'S MINE!"

Wrench lunges forward, and Marcus reaches his arms out and grabs onto Wrench's legs. Marcus spins Wrench around a few times by his legs, before letting go and watching Wrench fly through the air into a control panel on the wall. The panel sparks and the lights flicker as Wrench crumbles to the ground like a ragdoll. Janus kneels next to Simon, rolling him onto his back and freaking out.

"Simon! Wake up!" he yells. Simon's face remains static and unresponsive. He slaps Simon's face a few times until Marcus catches up and pushes Janus away. Marcus throws his hands down and rubs Simon's sternum. After a few rubs, Simon's eyes blink open. He groans in pain as he rolls around.

"OW!" he yells out. "What the hell did you do?"

"That doesn't matter, you need to get up NOW!" Marcus says as he and Janus pull Simon up by his arms. Simon gets to his feet and shakes his head a few times, and wipes sweat from his forehead.

"Where is Geno?" he asks.

"Over there," Marcus says, pointing to the portal, where Martin Geno has mysteriously disappeared. "Or he was."

"I'm right behind you," Geno says, from behind the three. They all turn their heads to see Geno towering over them, with Ron standing afar. "You know, you're pretty lucky to have a friend like Ron."

"Ron?" Simon asks.

"I found Ron in MY office trying to steal this," Geno says as he pulls out a vial from his suit's inside pocket. It's a small silver tube, with a flowing purple liquid inside. Bubbles flow around the vial. He shakes it around a few times, with a pissed expression.

"What is that?" Simon asks. "What do you have in your hand?"

Geno laughs, putting the vial back into his suit. He walks past the trio, patting Simon on the head and clacking his feet against the unfinished tile floor.

"It's just a cure I've been working on," Geno says. He walks up to the portal, putting his hand up to the flowing blue. "It'll stop Marcus from turning into one of those...freaks."

"What are you talking about?" Janus yells out. "You're talking bullshit."

"Oh!" Geno sarcastically gasps. "You mean he hasn't...TOLD you yet?"

"Told us WHAT?" Simon asks. He and Janus both look at Marcus, who steps backward. Ron walks over to them, but also keeps his distance. Marcus gulps as he scratches his left arm.

"That he's corrupted," Geno explains. "He'll turn into a freak any moment now."

Marcus pulls up his left sleeve, and the arm is almost to the bone. Purple streaks under his skin, and his muscle has turned to lavender, rock-like material. He looks down at the floor, ashamed of the corruption he got.

"Marcus!" Janus cries. "Why wouldn't you tell me?"

"I'm sorry Janus, I didn't want to worry you guys," Marcus quickly says.

"Anyway, because of YOU, Marcus, I had to kill Ron's mother," Geno says. He turns toward the others and laughs. "That creature you kicked in the chest? That was his mother. And I had to kill it to put it out of his misery."

Ron closes his eyes as his breathing deepens. Sweat drips down his face and arms. His greasy long hair covers his eyes.

"Isn't that right, Ron?" Geno asks. Ron hesitates, but reluctantly nods his head. "How about you go kill Marcus? He did SUCH a bad thing…and if you kill Marcus and the others, I'll let you live. And I'll even let your FATHER live."

"My father?" Ron asks. Geno nods like he's speaking to a child.

"Yes, Ron," he adds. "Your father is still alive, and he's with me on the other side. He's been looking for you. So just kill those three and you can see him again."

"Yes…sir," Ron says, turning his head toward the trio. Marcus raises his hands in defense, stepping backward toward the wall.

"Come on Ron," he says as Ron walks toward them, bending his fingers into veiny fists. His eyes break through his wall of hair as he lifts his head up. The green pupils blend into a red and yellow color.

"I can't lose my father," he growls. "You are all just loose ends to the CDD."

Ron runs forward at Marcus, who ducks as Ron dives forward, hitting a wall. Marcus runs over to Ron, kicking him a few times in the stomach. Ron groans with each impact. Ron grabs onto Marcus' leg from the ground, twisting it to the side, causing Marcus to crash onto the concrete below. Ron crawls onto Marcus, shoving his hand down Marcus' throat.

"Hm," Geno laughs. "Poor Ron…doesn't even realize I've already killed his father. The mentally ill are so easy to control."

"You're a monster," Simon yells in Geno's face. "What you're doing…should be outlawed."

"Please, Simon," Geno says, crossing his arms. "I'm just doing my job."

"No," Simon states, pushing a finger into Geno's chest. "I created this company to HELP people, not to kill.

That is ALL you."

"I am helping people, Simon," Geno says, slapping Simon's finger away. "Even if it means killing a few to save the many."

Marcus pukes in his mouth, all over Ron's fingers, and bites down hard. Ron screams in pain as he tries to pull his hand out, but Marcus' teeth cut into the bone. When Marcus lets go, Ron pulls his hand out, revealing a bleeding and vomit-covered hand with marks across the palm. He trembles and falls backward, and Marcus gets back up.

"Fine, if you think killing people to help others is ok, then what I'm gonna do is justified," Simon says. He reaches into his pants, pulling out a makeshift pistol, crafted from wood, tree sap, and containing leaf-ball ammo. He points it at Geno's head, keeping one eye closed. "You're sick, Geno. The only cure for you is death."

"Simon," Geno says with a smile. "Once you kill once, you never go back."

"I'm not killing someone," Simon yells. "I'm killing a monster."

He puts his finger on the trigger, quickly pulling it back as Geno slaps the weapon away. The bullet flies right past Geno's face, grazing his cheek, and blasting into the wall behind them. Simon looks at Geno in shock, taking a step backward and aiming the gun again. Geno dodges another bullet, lunging forward and throwing a punch right to Simon's gut. Simon hunches forward, holding onto his stomach.

Geno walks over, laughing as he looks down on Simon. Simon takes a deep breath and pushes his arm up, uppercutting Geno in the throat. His bottom jaw breaks through his upper jaw, and a few teeth fall out. Blood pools out of his mouth, and drips down his lower lip. He wipes the blood away, staring down Simon.

"Good one, bitch," Geno whispers. Simon points the gun up, right at Geno's forehead. Geno quickly reaches his arm out, slapping it out of Simon's hand. The gun slides across the ground, hitting the Portal Machine in the corner of the room. Simon screams at Geno, running forward and tackling him to the ground. Geno is crushed under Simon's weight, and the two begin a punching match.

Janus Peterson stares at the awakened Janus Wrench, who holds onto a bloody knife and stares through his golden mask. His limbs are slightly shorter than Peterson's, but his legs are longer. His white eyes never blink, and the crack in the golden mask bleeds a clear liquid.

"Who even are you?" Peterson asks.

"The man you replaced," Wrench answers. He holds up the knife toward Peterson.

"What are you even talking about?" Peterson asks. Wrench jumps forward, slashing at Peterson, but misses. Peterson dodges, punching Wrench in the spine. Wrench falls forward, almost stabbing himself with the knife.

"Don't act like you don't know who I am!" Wrench growls from the floor. Peterson stands over him.

"I don't know who you are!" Peterson yells from above. Wrench flips onto his stomach, staring up at Peterson.

"You are ME!" Wrench maniacally laughs.

"What?" Peterson asks.

"You're a fake, Peterson!" Wrench explains. "A copy! A doppelganger! You aren't real, I'm the real one!"

"No, that's not true. That's impossible!" Peterson exclaims, stepping backward. Peterson looks back at Simon, who is slamming Geno's face into the floor. Wrench takes the distraction to jump up and stab Peterson in the left shoulder. He screams as he puts his hand over the wound, falling to his knees.

Ron stands up with shaking legs. Marcus holds both hands up, ready to fight, as blood seeps from his nose. The blood has a purple tint to it.

"Come on, Ron, we don't have to fight," Marcus bargains. "We can just leave together."

"I told you already," Ron coughs. "I have to do this. I have no choice."

"There's always a choice," Marcus responds.

"Not against Geno."

"He's just a human, Ron!" Marcus yells. "He's not unbeatable."

"You wouldn't understand Marcus…," Ron cries

165

out. "You haven't seen the things he does…he's not a human. He's a monster who will do ANYTHING to get what he wants."

"Well, no matter what he is, he can't take us all on," Marcus says, reaching out a hand and lowering his fists. "If we team up, we can take Geno down."

"But what if we can't? What if he's too strong for all of us?" Ron asks. His lower lip bleeds from a cut on the inside.

"That's a risk that we'll have to take," Marcus responds. Ron nods. He walks toward Marcus, grabbing onto his hand. They both shake, and turn toward Geno punching Simon to the ground.

"You're right, Marcus," Ron says. "I don't want to go home if it means y'all can't come with me. We'll beat Martin Geno, get the cure, and get the hell out of here."

Geno punches Simon's face so hard, a tooth shoots out and Simon crashes to the floor. His face is covered in blood, and his cut eye gushes with pus. Simon coughs up blood as he struggles for breath, Geno wobbling over him. Geno reaches into his suit, pulling out a golden Millikin Colt Dragoon Revolver. He presses the end to Simon's forehead, as Simon tries to put up his hands in defense. Geno pulls down on the trigger as Marcus dives into Geno, knocking him and the gun down.

"Marcus?" Simon asks as he rolls to his side. Marcus drives a heavy fist into Geno's face, and kicks the gun away. Ron runs over to Simon, helping him to his feet.

"Barney?"

"It's Ron, remember?" Ron says. "Barney was just a front."

"Why did you switch sides?" Simon asks. Ron laughs and sighs.

"I'm tired of taking orders from a monster like Geno. I'm sorry for getting mad about you wanting to kill him. I don't know why, but I was just so scared of him," Ron explains to Simon. "I thought of him as some terrible God who punished all in his way, but he's human. Just like the rest of us. And that means he can be killed JUST like the rest of us."

"What are you saying, Ron?" Simon asks. Ron turns his head toward Geno, who pushes Marcus off him. Geno stands up before the portal, the bright blue and white light shining down on him.

"We kill that motherfucker Martin Geno once," Ron says. "And for all."

Marcus runs past Simon and Ron toward Janus. Geno holds out his arms.

"Are you both done talking?" he yells. "I'd like to say a few things."

"We don't care about what you have to say," Simon says. Geno shakes his head and laughs under his breath.

"Oh, no. I don't want to say anything to you guys. You are all talking about killing me, so before I die, I want to at least finish one last experiment. My biggest one yet," Geno says. "Project…"

"No, you can't be talking about-," Simon starts.

"Worlds Collide," Geno finishes. The wind in the room picks up, throwing everyone's hair around their heads.

"How do you plan on doing that? The Universal Combining Machine is back on our Earth, and we aren't going to let you back there alive," Ron states coldly. Geno laughs. He lowers his hands.

"Then, I guess I'll have to kill you before you kill me," Geno responds. Marcus reaches the two Janus', watching as Peterson sits on top of Wrench's back, slamming his face into the ground. Pieces of the mask shatter off, and blood stains the floor below. Wrench kicks himself up, knocking Peterson back. Marcus catches him before he falls down.

"Are you ok, Janus?" Marcus asks. Peterson shakes his arms.

"Yeah, I'm fine," Peterson says, patting Marcus on the shoulder. "I had that under control, for the most part."

"Ya, I'm sure you did," Marcus jokes. Peterson looks down to Wrench crawling away with broken legs. The knife he held lays on the ground, a few feet away from Wrench. Peterson walks past him, leaning over and picking the knife up. Wrench looks up with worry in his pupils.

"What are you going to do with that?" Wrench asks. Peterson chuckles.

"I'm going to kill myself," Peterson answers.

"What?" Marcus yells out. Peterson slowly takes

each step at a time, toward Wrench, who screams in panic. He tries to crawl away, quickly pulling himself along with both bleeding arms.

"Stay back!" Wrench yells. "Don't get near me!"

Peterson grabs onto Wrench's legs, pulling him back. Wrench sticks his nails in the floor, and as he's brought backward, his nails are ripped off.

"I said stay back!" he yells as Peterson flips him over. "Get away from me! Please!"

Peterson pulls Wrench under him, pinning him down with his arms. Peterson's eyes glow a deep red, and his neck bulges with veins. Wrench tries to push Peterson off, punching and slapping Peterson's body, but he is unmovable.

"Please!" Janus Wrench calls out. He throws his hands up in front of his face in defense. Janus Peterson holds the knife up, screaming as he grips the handle. "Don't do this! Please."

Janus Peterson's breath slows down and his arms slowly lower. He drops his arms down and places one of his hands on Wrench's chest. Wrench lets out a loud sigh of relief as Peterson slides the knife across Wrench's stomach, up to his throat. Wrench gasps as the knife slices through his throat, and Peterson drags it through Wrench's skin. Blood pours in his mouth and from his throat. Wrench's hands shoot up to his neck, trying to press down on his wounds. His eyes open wide and he gasps for breaths. The dark red blood spills out onto the floor, and

Peterson pulls the knife out. He looks down on the thick, jagged red line on Wrench's neck.

"What did I just do," Janus says, dropping the knife to his side. His hands are stained with blood. Marcus runs up to Janus, and kicks the knife away.

"You killed him," Marcus says, putting a hand on Janus' back. Wrench's arms drop to the ground as his chest stops beating. The white pupils behind his golden mask fade into black.

"I had to, he was going to kill me," Janus cries out.

"We need to go get Ron and Simon," Marcus says, grabbing Janus' arms and pulling him to his feet. Janus stumbles to gain his balance as his eyes water from the event before. Marcus pushes Janus along, and the two join with Simon and Ron.

"Now, you two are joining the fight," Geno exclaims. He brushes his suit as the wind flops his hair around. Simon growls and runs over to Geno, punching him in the face. Ron joins, and kicks Geno to the ground. Marcus grabs onto Geno's ears, pulling him up and kicking his face with his knee. Janus grabs onto his neck and punches his jaw. Simon drops Geno to the ground again, and pulls some patches of hair out. Janus kicks Geno in the eye, and drags him along the floor.

Ron screams as he pummels the back of Geno's head with a barrage of punches. Simon and Marcus lock arms and both fall backward on Geno's back. Marcus picks up Geno by his legs, lifting him up into the air and letting him drop down. Ron rubs his greasy hair into Geno's mouth, which causes him to sneeze and jump backward toward the portal. The four men stand their ground as Geno stands up. He struggles, gaining his balance after a few seconds of falling.

"You…think you've defeated me?" Geno yells through bloody teeth. "Huh?"

"Why do you sound like a stereotypical villain? Janus asks. In a mocking tone, he copies Geno's line. "You think you have defeated me? Oh, I'm Martin Geno, a big, fat, ugly, loser-ass bitch."

"You think you're funny, huh?" Geno yells. His voice echoes through the chamber. "Let's see how FUNNY you think you are when I destroy THIS."

Geno reaches into his suit, pulling out the cure. It shines from the light behind them. He wiggles it around, and the group all gasp.

"You all need to understand something," Geno screams out loud. "When I met Simon, he was a good man. But when we started this company, he went money crazy. I tried to protect Simon, but he pushed me away. So I pushed him to another place in space."

"You think you protected me?" Simon laughs. "You really think that?"

"How did you get infected, Marcus?" Geno asks. "Do tell."

"I'm not too sure…," Marcus says. Janus looks over at him. "I think it's when I kicked a doppelganger and something slithered into my shoe."

"And if we don't get that cure, he will die," Simon growls. "We need to kill Geno."

"A little too late to kill me, don't you think?" Geno laughs.

"Geno, please give us the cure," Janus tries to bargain. "We'll do anything, I'll do anything, just please help Marcus."

"No, Janus, don't even try. You don't know what you're getting yourself into," Ron says, cutting off Janus' words. Geno puts his fingers on his chin, rubbing it and thinking.

"Hm…," Geno thinks for a moment. "You know, that is a good deal."

He walks over to Janus, holding out the cure with a smile. Janus smiles back, reaching his hard out and almost touching the cure.

"But I think I'll pass," Geno says. He drops the cure to the ground before Janus can grab it. As if in slow motion, Janus watches the vial shatter on the ground, with glass and purple liquid splashing everywhere. Janus steps backward in shock, unable to speak or take his eyes off the mess.

"Well, I think it's time for me to go," Geno says. He takes a few steps backward, and watches as a random guard runs into the room from the exit door. The guard wears a light blue collared shirt and black pants. He opens a panel door on the Portal Machine, pushing a few buttons as Geno walks backward into the portal. "Enjoy your lives, gentlemen. Except Marcus, I guess."

He backs through the portal, and as he disappears, it flashes a few times before closing. A few seconds go by, and then it reopens, but this time a little smaller. Janus drops to his knees, with his mouth open wide and Marcus stands behind him. Marcus closes his eyes, accepting his fate.

"Come on guys, we need to follow him!" Simon yells. He runs toward the portal, and Ron helps Janus up as they do the same. The guard at the panel picks up Simon's makeshift gun, putting the barrel up to his neck and killing himself. Blood splatters the wall behind him, and his head disconnects from his neck and falls to the ground. Marcus wobbles as he runs, and he holds onto his left arm and screams in pain. Janus stops right before the barrier, looking back at Marcus as he struggles to catch up. Janus looks back at Simon and Ron, who stop as well. Marcus stomps his feet, but slips on a wet spot and crashes to the ground. He falls face first, and the sound of his skull cracking against the concrete floor echoes through the chamber.

"Marcus!" Janus yells out. He runs over to Marcus, pushing him onto his back. Blood runs from Marcus' nose, and pools around his left eye, which is completely closed. "We need to go! We need to get you a cure!"

"Janus!" Simon yells out. Janus grabs onto Marcus' arms, pulling him across the harsh floor. He struggles due to Marcus' weight, and pulls as hard as he can.

"Someone come help me!" Janus cries out. "PLEASE!"

Ron jogs over and grabs onto Marcus' legs, trying to lift him up and push as Janus pulls. He has a harder time than Janus. The chamber shakes, and a few clumps of rock crumble from the ceiling. The barrier cracks, and shrinks by a few feet. Simon notices, and takes a step closer.

"Hurry, guys!" he yells. "The portal is closing!"

"Leave...me," Marcus says through a broken jaw. "I can feel myself...turning."

"No, no, no," Janus says, pulling harder than before. They're only a few yards away from the portal as rock above the entrance door slides off the walls, blocking the exit. The lights above flicker on and off, and the only other light is the blue glow from the portal. "I can't leave you here, you need to come home with us."

Marcus coughs up some blood, which stains Janus' arms.

"I'm sorry Janus," Marcus whispers. "I can't be here for you."

"No, don't say that," Janus says. He turns his head toward the portal, which pulses and blue streaks fall from the middle. He can see his reflection in the sparkling light, and can barely make out the woods on the other side. He turns back to Marcus. "I need you, man. You're all I got."

"Janus," Marcus says. "Please stop. I need you to leave."

"No," Janus states. Marcus turns his arms around, and Janus' grip loosens. Marcus falls down, hitting his head against the floor again as the crumbling purple rocks and cracks reach his neck. His eyes turn a soft lavender glow, and his pupils disappear. Janus tries to grab onto Marcus' arms again, but Ron grabs Janus and pulls him back. "GET OFF ME!"

"JANUS!" Ron yells into Janus' ear. He pushes Janus toward the portal. "GO!"

"NO!" Janus yells. "I won't leave him here!"

"Janus," Simon says, walking over to him. He grabs onto Janus' shoulders, holding him back. A gust of wind blows into the room from the portal, and causes the room to shake once more.

"Take him through," Ron says to Simon. Janus' head jumps from the shock of what he hears. Janus looks back to Simon, who tightens his grip on Janus' shoulders. "Now."

Simon nods, and picks up Janus and puts him over his shoulder. Janus screams at the top of his lungs as he pounds his fists on Simon's back. Simon walks into the closing portal, which sends out a shockwave that shatters some of the lights above. Glass falls to the ground, nearly slicing through Marcus.

"I'm sorry, Marcus," Ron says. "For betraying you. For everything."

Marcus smiles as he sits on the floor. The corruption reaches the bottom of his neck, and little purple crumbs fall from his face. He laughs to himself as he pulls his sleeve up to reveal his arm has been withered down to the bone. His cloudy eyes look up to Ron.

"Don't apologize. I get it," he says with a smile. "Just…take care of Janus for me. Ok?"

Ron nods his head, turning around and walking toward the portal. Marcus coughs before Ron walks through, and he turns around.

"One…more thing," Marcus says, holding up a finger. He points to his head with two fingers, and lowers his thumb. Ron nods his head in understanding. He reaches into his back pocket, where he has an 1847 Colt Walker Revolver, which was a gift from his grandfather. "I don't want to turn."

"I…can't," Ron says. "It doesn't feel right."

"I want you to, Ron," Marcus says. "It's either you kill me now, or I suffer for longer."

"I…," Ron starts. He doesn't say another word. He closes his eyes, and aims the revolver at Marcus' head. Marcus closes his eyes as well, and takes a final breath.

Janus waits eagerly against a tree. He bites his nails, watching the blue orb in the middle of the clearing shrink more and more. Simon sits on the ground, laying his legs across some tree roots. Ron comes through the portal, bursting through the blue orb. It pulses behind him as he falls to his knees in the wet dirt. The orb flashes for a few seconds before suddenly disappearing. Janus runs up to Ron.

"Where is he?" Janus yells out. Ron closes his eyes and lowers his head. "Ron, answer me. WHERE IS HE?"

"That…doesn't matter right now," Ron sighs. "We need to go find Geno and stop him."

"Are you serious right now?" Janus screams. "Marcus is somewhere out there in the universe, and all you care about is finding Geno? Did you not CARE about him AT ALL?"

"Janus, calm down," Simon butts in. "We all cared about him, but finding Geno is what's important right now?"

"IMPORTANT?" Janus yells, turning his head quickly toward Simon. Janus' watery eyes shine, and a tear rolls down his right cheek. "You can't be serious. This is all YOUR fault. YOU wanted to kill Geno. YOU'RE the reason we're here in the first place."

"He would've died no matter what," Simon coldly states. "He was infected. Corrupted."

"And whose fault is that? If it weren't for you and your shitty science labs, those stupid portals wouldn't still be around," Janus continues.

"Those portals brought you back," Simon says. Janus screams at him.

"SHUT UP!" Janus kicks the ground, sending a pile of dirt and grass through the air. "If we never went through that portal, he would still be here. Here with US.

Alive."

"Well, you're still alive, aren't you?" Simon exclaims. "Now he's dead, and there's nothing you can do about it. So why don't you stop your whining. We need to go and find Geno."

"Janus," Ron says from next to him. "Simon is right. We need to find Geno before he kills us all. One sacrifice can lead to the entire population staying alive."

"Who cares about his plans?" Janus yells. He's less aggressive and agitated now, and instead sounds saddened and empty.

"Project Worlds Collide will kill everyone if it fails," Ron says. "And will kill everyone if it goes through."

"At this point, I don't care," Janus says. He falls to the ground on his ass, laying back onto the mud. He lays his arms out and stares up through the tree. He closes his eyes as tears stream down.

"Feeling sorry for yourself isn't what Marcus would have wanted. He wouldn't want you to stop caring about everyone and everything, just because he's gone," Ron explains. He stands up next to Janus.

"You barely even knew him," Janus cries from the ground. He covers his eyes with his muddy hands.

"I know enough about him to know that he wouldn't want you to be acting like this," Ron says. "We need to go save everyone, Janus. Geno is threatening everything."

"It's not fair," Janus cries. "Why did HE have to go?"

Ron sighs. He places a hand on Janus' forehead.

"Nothing is fair," Ron explains. "You just have to accept it and move on. He might be gone, but that doesn't mean you have to give up on everything. You need to create a life that he would be PROUD of. He'd want us to kill Martin Geno, and save the fucking world."

"I guess you're right," Janus says, wiping his eyes. He takes a deep breath and sits up. Simon walks over, and helps Janus up. "Let's go find this bastard."

"I agree," Ron says. Simon nods his head, and the three begin their adventure through the forest, toward Janus' old neighborhood. The sun shines down on them, casting the land in a soft yellow light. The orange and green leaves wave in the wind, and the smell of pie fills the air.

—

- December 24th, 2000 -

Janus Peterson knocks at the cabin door of Simon Wrench. He waits at the door for a moment, wearing a heavy black fur coat, white gloves, and a comfortable wool hat. The woods around the cabin look exactly like the ones in the other world, but there is no hill, and the ground is mostly flat. The leaves are coating in a nice coat of white snow, and a few flakes drop from the sky. The door opens, and an older Simon Wrench stands in the doorway. His hair has a few strands of gray throughout, and he wears an unwashed white tank top, and dirty jeans.

"Can I come in?" Janus asks. Simon nods and waves forward.

"Oh yes, here, come on in," Simon says as he holds the door open. They walk through some dark rooms to the table of five seats, where Simon takes the broken chair. "It's just like the other world."

"Just without the hill," Janus laughs. He takes a seat on the table opposite Simon.

"Any progress with finding Geno?" Simon asks. "We had him in our grasp and he got away…I'm not sure if we'll ever get that close to him again. At least not without Ron and your help."

"What about you?" Janus asks. "What about your help?"

Simon sighs and shakes his head.

"You know I can't help," he says. "I have a family again, I can't risk losing them."

"I understand, Simon," Janus says with a smile. "How's your daughter doing? I haven't seen her since she was born."

"She's getting pretty big," Simon laughs. "She's walking now, so that's good."

"Last time we talked, you and Mary couldn't decide on a name," Janus says. "Have you chosen one yet?"

"Yes. Her name is Janx."

"That's…an interesting name," Janus says slowly. "Is it after your son, Janus?"

"Yes," Simon responds.

"It's a good name." Janus nods his head and smiles at Simon. "Anyway, I should be going. Ron and I are going out of town for a bit."

Janus stands up, and Simon follows. They both walk to the front door, where Janus steps out into the snowy grass. Flakes fall from the sky in large quantities, and they lay softly against the ground. Janus puts his hands in his coat pockets, turning back to Simon before he leaves.

"Thank you Simon. For everything."

Simon smiles.

"If you ever need anything, Janus, don't hesitate to come to me," Simon says. He gives a quick wave as Janus walks out the door. The wood creaks as it opens, and Simon stands in the doorway holding the door open with his right arm. His cut eye has gotten better, but he insists on wearing a pirate-like eyepatch over it. The howling wind screams as the trees shake. "Take care of yourself."

"You too, Simon," Janus ends with as he walks into the flurry of snow. He disappears into the white fog, and Simon walks back into the house. The door closes with a slam, and the sun sets on another beautiful day.

24

Worlds Collide

A siren wails through the cleared out halls of the CDD. The gray linoleum floors reflect the buzzing fluorescent yellow lights that illuminate the wooden brown walls. Past one of the two-way metal doors, Martin Geno leans over a circular screen. Behind him, a female scientist holds a clipboard close to her chest. Geno blocks her out of his vision. He is only focused on the screen, which displays two globe shapes.

"Project Worlds Collide initiated," a robotic female voice echoes from loudspeakers around the small room. Other scientists watch on from their desks. The only light in the room shines white down upon Geno's black suit. "Starting up Universal Collision Machine."

"Sir, are you sure we should be doing this?" the female scientist asks. "The U.C.M. tests only had a 63% chance of success. If this fails, everyone might die and that will include you."

Geno chuckles as his eyes stay glued to the screen. Blood rushes to his unblinking pupils, and his eyes begin to dry.

"I am sure this will work. Simon Wrench's research will prove to be the drive for my Nobel Peace Prize," Geno coldly states.

"Collision in 5…," the robot voice calls out. The globes on the screen begin to move closer to each other.

"This will work," Geno says once more.

"4."

The female scientist looks at her clipboard and flips through the papers, sweat dripping down her face.

"3."

A sudden shake rushes through the room. The scientist falls to her knees, yet Geno remains unmoved.

"2."

The shaking begins again, yet this time it does not yield. People fall, computers crash to the ground, but Geno remains standing over the table.

"1."

The light above Geno dismantles from the ceiling as cracks form in the walls. It slams down into the screen, finally breaking Geno's concentration. He looks up at the debris and destruction the merging has caused. He wipes a puddle of dust from his left shoulder, and adjusts his tie.

"Collision successful."

"Sir…," the female scientist says, climbing to her feet. "It worked. You actually did it, you successfully merged two dimensions together."

Geno smiles as she flips through papers again.

"The doppel-creating effects of the other world will

now be applied to ours…and our Earth can spawn doppelgangers," she exclaims. Everyone in the room cheers; throwing papers up, hugging each other, even screaming bloody-murder. However, Geno remains stoic.

"I want everyone in this building to begin prep work on Operation: See Double immediately," he yells.

"Sir," one of the male scientists asks from across the room. His computer sparks underneath a chunk of concrete ceiling. "Don't you want to celebrate this victory?"

"Victory should be celebrated if it was not assured from the beginning," Geno responds. "And I believe I said immediately. Clean off your desks and begin working."

"Yes sir, sorry sir," the man responds. He turns and attempts to pick up the debris. A few other scientists pull out papers from filing cabinets throughout the room. Geno slowly walks out, and down the hallway.

He enters a small room, where a singular scientist sits on a rolling chair. Not Dr. Peterson. He rolls around the rectangular space, flipping levers and pushing buttons on different control panels. A large one-way window peers into a claustrophobic call, where a bandaged person lays on a bed. An IV and heart-rate monitor sit on either side. The monitor beeps at a slow fifty BPM.

"What did you say this person's name was?" Geno asks. "And how did you get them?"

"We found 'em in the doppel world forest," the scientist explains. He speaks with a lit cigarette in his mouth. "Name's Janus Wrench. You had a run-in with him before. I think he could be useful for Operation: See Double."

"Perfect," Geno says. "Prepare the mask."

25

Taken

- October 30th, 2007 -

Simon runs through the woods, something following quickly behind him. He tries to outrun the creature, but his big legs limit him. A giggling voice echoes through the dense trees, and the smog hides whatever is behind him.

He can see the soft yellow light of his cabin in the distance as his foot is caught on a twisting vine. He yells out as he slams into the mud. He looks up to see two stubby legs wearing bright yellow rain boots.

"Caught you!" a young girl calls out. Simon smiles as he picks himself up. He grabs onto the girls and hoists her onto his right shoulder.

"Yes you did!" he says, giving the girl a high-five. "What do you think momma made for dinner? And what do you think she's gonna think of all this mud?"

"Momma's gonna be mad!" the girl yells out. Her short, straight black hair waves in the wind and her bright green eyes match her mother's.

"Yes she will!" Simon laughs. He begins to walk toward his home, where he can see the silhouette of his wife waiting for him at the sliding glass door on the ground floor. He feels a droplet of rain on his nose, which causes his face to scrunch up.

They're only a few yards away when a figure walks out from behind a curving black tree. A man in a crisp black suit with his arms behind his back steps across a few leaves and blocks the way to Simon's home. He instantly recognizes the man as Martin Geno.

"Nice to see you again, Simon," Geno says with a bitchy smirk. Simon lowers his daughter to the ground, and she grabs onto his gray sweater and hides behind him. Another drop of water falls onto his face. "Finding you was difficult, but it still happened."

"Geno. What do you want," he yells out. Geno claps as a few masked men cast in shadow appear from other trees. "What is the meaning of this?"

"I just wanted to see my BEST FRIEND in the whole wide WORLD's child!" Geno says with a shrug. He walks a few feet toward Simon, and leans over to be eye level with Simon's daughter. "What a cute one, isn't she?"

He eyes Simon, who keeps a firm arm in front of her. A few more droplets of rain fall down, a few even cutting right through fallen leaves.

"Geno, I'm done going after you," Simon says, standing his ground. "Leave me and my family alone."

Geno laughs as he stands right up. He raises his hands up in a defensive stance and takes a step back. He shakes his head.

"Don't worry, I'm going to leave you and your wife

alone, do not worry."

Geno notices Simon's firm arm loosen a little.

"But I'm not finished with you yet," he adds. Two men drop down from the covering trees and topple Simon to the ground. He falls with a heavy grunt and his daughter yells out his name as another two shadowy figures grab onto her arms. "How old is she? Eight? Nine?"

"What is the meaning of this?" Simon yells out from the ground, the two men holding his arms behind his back. He struggles to move around as the men are big in muscle. Geno steps over and places his shining dress shoes on either side of Simon's head.

"I thought you could be a good partner, and you were," Geno scoffs. He checks out his nails on both hands as he talks. "But you were always better than me. Both in brains and morally."

"Why are you taking her?" Simon cries. The shadowy figures drag his daughter into the smog as her cries are muffled by their hands.

"It's time for Martin Geno to go public," Geno explains. "I've been overshadowed by your accomplishments, even after your 'death.' And who doesn't love a family man?"

"Take me! Leave her and take me, you fucking DICK SUCKER!" Simon yells out. Geno places one of his feet onto Simon's head and pushes it into the mud.

"Oh Simon, don't worry. I won't hurt a single hair on her body, you can trust me on that. She'll be under my protection, I'll treat her as if she were my own daughter," Geno laughs. "That is the whole point."

"I'll come back for you," Simon says from the ground. His voice is muffled from the mouthful of mud. Geno wipes his foot on Simon's hair and lets go. The men jump backward and disappear into the smog. Geno looks down at Simon's defeated demeanor.

"I'm sure you will."

Geno walks away, disappearing behind the same tree he came out from. Simon looks at his house as an orange light illuminates his face. A flame rages on from the inside of his wooden cabin. His wife's burns as the crackling of flames echoes through the forest. Simon lays defeated as the flames rage on, both in his house and inside his heart.

26

Road Trip

A television lays on top of a brick fireplace. The room is warm, and the abstract art on the white walls gives it a modernized look. On the left side of the room, a black wooden desk rests under a silver 2015 MacBook Pro. In the middle of the room, a brown leather couch seats two boys, both about to turn eighteen. They watch the television, which displays a news show.

"The whole family was murdered, suspects are few and far between, yada-yada-yada," a reporter says in a could-care-less voice. He shuffles some papers around as he suits in a black suit that matches his dark short hair. He pushes up some rectangular glasses, and continues. "Thoughts and prayers to the family, or whatever. Anyways, a new six-ten curfew will be in place, and now over to Ted with the Interview of the Day."

The view switches to an aged Ted Krinks, in his usual orange suit, sits on a swivel hand chair, and speaks to an estranged couple. They both sit on a park bench, although the interview is taking place inside a subway bathroom. Ted gives them both a microphone, and leans back in his chair.

"We are here, today, with a couple who are from Utah, and have been traveling all across the United States for what they call the All-Around Road Trip," Ted explains to the camera in a stuffy voice. "Now tell me, why?"

The man on the left starts, and his fluffy brown hair covers his wide, circular glasses. His large nose protrudes from between the lenses. He wears a Rammstein t-shirt, basketball shorts, and a Spongebob watch.

"Oh, it was something that I thought of because of the new year and new president being announced any day now," he says. His voice is high-pitched and slightly annoying. His wife next to him looks at him with a weird look. Her sparkling red hair makes her light blue eyes pop. She wears a black California shirt and a bracelet with an 'L' on it.

"Your idea?" she yells at him with a beautiful voice. "Bitch, that was MY idea!"

The couple argues as the two boys on the couch laugh at each other. The boy on the left, Jason Clay, is a tall, tan-colored Italian with dark stubble, brown eyes, and an overbite. The boy on the right, Mark Peterson, is a thick, American with a brown bowl-cut, flabby cheeks, and a covered forehead.

"Dude, wouldn't that be fun?" Mark laughs in a deep voice. He rests his arms on his large stomach.

"Dude, I have an idea," Jason responds in a higher, but still heavy voice. "You thinking what I'm thinking?"

The two boys look at each other, smiling with wide mouths. They both nod a few times, and in sync the boys yell out what they're thinking.

"ROAD TRIP!"

ABOUT THE AUTHOR

 Lucas Brady lives in the United States, enjoying writing his weirdass stories and sharing them with friends. He enjoys sleeping, playing *Five Nights at Freddy's*, and drawing (sometimes). He hates writing straight non-fiction, but will do as much research as he can to implement real-world events within his fictional stories. He's published four standalone books before the age of 18, and will continue until he dies.

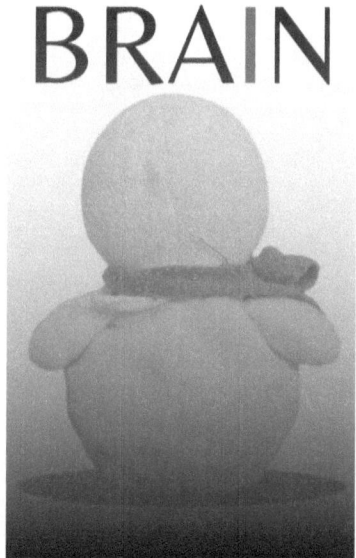